NORMA CHARLES

RAINCOAST BOOKS

Vancouver

Raincoast Books acknowledges the ongoing financial support of the Government of Canada through The Canada Council for the Arts and the Book Publishing Industry Development Program (BPIDP); and the Government of British Columbia through the BC Arts Council.

Edited by Lynn Henry
Text design by Ingrid Paulson

NATIONAL LIBRARY OF CANADA CATALOGUING IN PUBLICATION DATA

Charles, Norma M.
   All the way to Mexico / Norma Charles. — 1st ed.

   ISBN 1-55192-598-2

   I. Title.
PS8555.H4224A63 2003   jC813'.54   C2002-911402-0
PZ7.C42724AL 2003

LIBRARY OF CONGRESS CONTROL NUMBER: 2002096039

Raincoast Books   *In the United States:*
9050 Shaughnessy Street   Publishers Group West
Vancouver, British Columbia   1700 Fourth Street
Canada   V6P 6E5   Berkeley, California
www.raincoast.com   94710

At Raincoast Books we are committed to protecting the environment and to the responsible use of natural resources. We are acting on this commitment by work-ing with suppliers and printers to phase out our use of paper produced from ancient forests. This book is one step towards that goal. It is printed on 100% ancient-forest-free paper (40% post-consumer recycled), processed chlorine- and acid-free, and supplied by New Leaf paper. It is printed with vegetable-based inks. For further information, visit our website at www.raincoast.com. We are working with Markets Initiative (www.oldgrowthfree.com) on this project.

Printed in Canada by Webcom.

10 9 8 7 6 5 4 3 2 1

With love to Jason, Melanie, Andrea, Michael, Colin,
and especially Brian, who were on the first trip, all the way to Mexico

I

Jacob Armstrong was twelve years old and he was on a honeymoon. The honeymoon was his mother's.

Also on the honeymoon was his mother's new husband, Fred Finkle.

They'd been married just the day before.

To make matters crazier, Jacob's fifteen-year-old sister Minerva was on the honeymoon as well. And so were Fred Finkle's two kids, Barney Finkle, who was ten, and Sam Finkle, eight. They were all packed together in a car.

There were three Finkles and three Armstrongs in the car, except that Jacob's mother wasn't an Armstrong any longer. Now she was Rosalina *Finkle*. Which made it *four* Finkles, not three, Jacob suddenly realized. And only *two* Armstrongs. It was like losing his mother. Like those Finkles had stolen her away.

The car was a temperamental old Mercury Montego station wagon. Pale blue. Musty smelling. It even had a name. They called it "Big Blue." On its roof was a kayak and a long storage box that Minerva and her friends had painted with green, gold and red stripes, Jamaican Rastafarian colours. Jacob had glued a big soccer ball sticker on the end.

Fred Finkle was driving and Jacob's mother sat beside him up front. Minerva sat beside her next to the door.

Jacob had to sit in the back, sandwiched between the two Finkle brothers. He was a Finkle sandwich and he was totally fed up. Especially since Barney Finkle wouldn't stop with his stupid cow jokes.

"Okay," Barney said, pushing up his glasses and licking his lips. "Let me try this one out on you again."

Jacob groaned inwardly and stared past Barney's pointy freckled nose, out the window at the blur of highway traffic. They were on their way to Mexico. It was a Mexican honeymoon for six.

They had left Vancouver early that morning, crossing the Canada/U.S. border at the Peace Arch. They travelled down the I-5 highway and sailed over Seattle and Tacoma on the overpasses, then they got tangled in Portland's criss-crossing octopus freeways at rush hour. After a long tunnel through a hill with a sprinkling of houses on top, they had turned west to follow the signs to the Oregon beaches. Now it was late afternoon and it was raining. Barney Finkle had hardly stopped talking to Jacob.

"Okay," Barney Finkle said again, clearing his throat and wiggling his butt farther into his seat. "So there's this guy, see. He's out riding his horse and he gets lost, see.

He meets this old woman leading a cow down the road. So he says, 'Excuse me, Ma'am. Can you tell me how to get to Morrisville?'

"Before the woman answers, the cow says, 'You go down the road about a mile, take the left fork, then you'll see the town right ahead. You can't miss it.'

"Well, the man's astonished, see. 'That's amazing!' he says. 'That cow told me how to get to Morrisville.'

"'What's so amazing about that?' the old woman says. 'She's lived here all her life.'"

Jacob groaned again, aloud this time, and bounced his soccer ball on his knee. It was at least the fifth time that day Barney Finkle had tried out the same oldy mouldy joke on him. And it wasn't even funny the first time.

"That was better, right?" Barney said, spraying Jacob in his excitement. "I added the bit about Morrisville. Good name for a town, right?"

"Sure, sure," Jacob said, wiping his cheek with the back of his hand. He rubbed his chin on his soccer ball. It felt smooth and cool. How he wished he could be out in some field somewhere, anywhere, kicking his ball around!

His mother said, "Fred, sweet, don't you think we should stay in a motel on such a wet night?"

"Motel?" Fred Finkle said. "A waste of money for just a few hours' sleep. I know an excellent state park just south of here where we can pitch our tents. And it'll cost us just ten dollars."

Jacob's mother shook her head but she didn't say anything else.

Frugal Fred Finkle, Jacob thought.

Barney Finkle flipped through his tattered joke book, *One Million Laughs*. "Hey! How about this one?" he said. "Why did the cow cross the road twice and refuse to take a bath?"

"I don't know," Jacob shrugged, stifling a yawn. "Why?"

"Because she was a dirty double-crosser."

"Hmm," Jacob mumbled. "Very funny."

"You really think so? Really? Maybe I should start my routine with that one. It *is* pretty funny, right? Dirty double-crosser. Ha!"

"Sure. Why not? But what do you want a routine for anyway?"

"Hey, you know how much stand-up comedians make? Plenty! And I want to be rich when I grow up. So to break in, I've got to have a sure-fire routine. And I thought I'd do one on cows. There's really nothing funnier than cows, right? Unless it's pigs. But I haven't come across that many jokes about pigs. But pigs would be pretty funny too, right?"

When Jacob didn't answer, Barney wiped the mist off the car window and consulted his joke book again in the dim light. "Okay, here's another one for you: 'My cow's got three speeds. Slow, slower and Here-comes-hamburger.' Oh, that's a good one! I like that! Get it? Slow, slower and Here-comes-hamburger!"

"Yeah, yeah," Jacob said. "Reminds me. I'm starving."

"Me too. When are we stopping for supper, Dad?"

Barney's father didn't hear him. He was too busy gabbing away to Jacob's mom.

"Da-ad," Barney said louder. "We're all starving back here."

"All right, all right, Barney-boy. We'll be stopping soon. Just a few more miles to Van Duzer State Park."

"How about a peppermint?" Jacob's mother said. She passed back a small bag of candies.

Jacob took one and handed the bag to Barney who also took one. When Jacob gave the bag to Sam, he stuck in his whole fist and ripped the bag.

"Jeeees!" Jacob muttered, grabbing at the candies as they tumbled to the cluttered floor. He found only a couple under Sam's grotty sandals. He wiped them off on his T-shirt and dropped them back into the crumpled bag.

When he handed the bag forward to his sister, Minerva, she grunted, "Gee, thanks for leaving us a couple."

"Not my fault," Jacob said. "Sam dumped them out."

"Don't you worry," his mother said. "We can buy more when we stop."

The peppermint tasted cool and sweet. Jacob wanted it to last as long as possible so he held it against the roof of his mouth with his tongue. Fat raindrops splattered on the windshield and the wipers went tick-swoosh, tick-swoosh, tick-swoosh. He bounced his ball against his knee in time with the wipers.

"Bet you haven't heard this one," Barney said. "How many cows does it take to change a light bulb?"

Jacob continued bouncing. Maybe if he ignored Barney, he would stop.

"None," Barney said finally. "The milk maid does it."

Jacob nodded but kept his mouth shut and watched one fat raindrop chase another down the windshield.

"Guess that one's not all that funny," Barney said. His glasses misted up and he wiped them with his fingers. "I'll have to think up some other answer."

"Why do you have to? Why don't you just sit back and relax?"

"If you want to be a good comedian, you have to practise every chance you get. Know what I mean? You ever heard of practise makes perfect?"

"Sure." Jacob rested his chin on his ball. Maybe jokes to Barney were like soccer was to him. To become a really good player, you had to practise all the time, that's for sure.

With Barney's looks, thought Jacob, becoming a comedian was probably his best bet. Besides wearing thick, wire-rimmed glasses, Barney had bristly red hair, freckles, and ears that stuck out like cup handles. Just looking at him made Jacob want to snicker. Nerd of the herd. Geek of the week.

In fact the whole Finkle family was funny looking. Sam Finkle was a smaller version of his brother, without the glasses and red hair. His hair was blond and had a tendency to stick up in the back.

Fred Finkle, the dad, was tall and skinny with a large red nose, bristly beard and knobby knees like Captain

Haddock in the Tintin comics. With his English accent, he sounded like Captain Haddock too.

"So let me try out that Morrisville one on you again," Barney said. "I've got it! I'll change the town to Clarabelle. Yeah, I like the sound of that. Has a real good ring to it. Clarabelle. Get it? Bell? Ring?"

Jacob stared straight ahead and concentrated on ignoring the kid. But Barney went on anyway.

"Okay, so there's this man, see. And one day, he's out riding his horse and gets lost, see. And he meets an old woman who's …"

Jacob gritted his teeth and ran his fingernails through his curly hair. Would the kid ever take a rest?

"Van Duzer State Park!" Minerva announced. "Sign says to turn right here."

Fred turned the station wagon off the highway and they bounced along a dark narrow road through a tunnel of wet trees. Branches reached out and scratched the side of the car like long pointy cow horns.

2

"Blimey! This is some downpour!" Fred Finkle said, backing the car into a vacant campsite beside a heavy picnic table that was sleek with rain. It was dark under the thick trees. "First item on our agenda will be setting up the tents."

While Fred rummaged in the back of the station wagon for camping equipment, Jacob followed Barney out into the wet evening. At least the kid had stopped with the cow jokes. He pulled his jacket on over his head and shivered, staring at the dripping trees and the soggy ground. "I'm sleeping in the car," he announced.

"Me too," Sam piped up.

"No, I am," Barney said.

"Nonsense," Fred said. "No one sleeps in the car. Why do you think we brought along these tents? Here. This one's for you and Sam." He handed Barney a bundle. "You should know how to set it up yourselves. And I can show you and Minerva how to set up yours," he said, giving Jacob another bundle.

"It's okay," Jacob said. "We've set up tents before. Want to grab the poles, Min?"

In his heart, he agreed with his mom. Staying in a motel made a lot more sense on this miserable wet night. He dumped the tent out of its nylon sack and spread it out on a level spot behind the car, near where Barney was setting up his. He'd gone camping a few times with the Scouts and this tent looked like the same kind they had used. A plain "A" frame with three poles, one for the front and one for the back, and another for the ridge. He held the fabric stiff while Minerva threaded the ridge pole through a narrow sleeve.

Meanwhile, Barney was trying to boss around his little brother. "Okay, Squirt. Don't just stand there. Grab an end of the tent."

Sam was standing beside the car with his hands full of toy action figures. He stared blankly at Barney as if to say, "Who are you talking to? Me?"

"Hey, Squirt. Come on," Barney grumbled. "Hustle! I'm getting all soaked out here."

Sam looked around for a place to stash his toys. Barney impatiently shook out the tent and flicked one of the toys out of his brother's hand.

"Hey, watch it!" Sam squealed. "That's Seraptor. My best one."

"Look. Just grab the end of the tent so we can set this thing up before we get totally soaked."

"But you made me lose my Seraptor." Sam kicked through the bushes. "I've got to find him."

Jacob and Minerva quickly finished pitching their tent so they could help Barney. Jacob stomped the tent pegs into the soft ground while Minerva installed the centre ridge pole that held up the roof.

"Come and have some supper, fellows," Jacob's mother called from the tent Fred and she were sharing. "Hot soup and buns sound good?"

"Yum," Jacob said, leading the way into the larger tent. Barney and Minerva followed him, while Sam stayed behind, searching for his toy in the dark bushes.

Jacob's mother was by the entrance stirring a pot of steaming soup over a small camp stove beside a lantern that gave off a warm golden glow.

"These camp stoves are excellent," Fred told them as they settled around inside the tent on foam mats. "Not only for these rainy conditions, but for ordinary dry days as well. There's less pollution, no ashes, burns no trees. But we must always be extra careful using them in the tent."

Jacob nodded as he leaned against his ball. Now we're going to get the "Safety-in-Our-Environment" lecture, he thought.

While Fred talked away, mainly to Barney, Jacob took a deep breath and inhaled the delicious smell of the chili bean soup. His stomach growled. He loved his mom's hot and spicy Jamaican cooking. Although they had lived in Canada for almost ten years now, since moving from

Jamaica when Jacob was just three, his mom still cooked good spicy Jamaican food.

Minerva sat beside Jacob and tried to stick a lighted candle into a metal camp-candle holder. Weird shadows flickered on the tent walls.

"Could you please pass around these bowls?" Jacob's mom asked him. As he handed a steaming bowl of soup to Barney, and one to Fred, Sam's head poked its way into the tent. The rain had plastered his blond hair flat, but he was grinning.

"I found him!" he said, holding up his toy. "I found my Seraptor."

"Good for you, Sam," Jacob's mom said. "Come now and have a bowl of this nice hot soup."

"Holy cow!" Barney exploded, lunging across the tent. He grabbed the water jug and took a long swig straight from it.

"Barnaby Finkle! Use your cup!" Fred said. He took a sip of his soup. "Ooooh my! This is bloomin' hot!" he exclaimed. "Hand over that water!" He grabbed the jug and gulped straight from it as well.

"Oh dear," Jacob's mom said. "Did I make the soup too spicy for you again? I always forget that you're not used to such highly seasoned dishes."

"No, no!" Fred said, coughing into his large red hand-kerchief. "It's tasty, very tasty. Just catches the back of the throat a bit." He sloshed more water into his cup and gulped it down, then blew his nose.

"Try some of this bread with it," Jacob's mom said with a worried frown.

Fred and Barney grabbed a couple of buns each and stuffed them into their mouths, spraying crumbs down their shirts.

Jacob felt like laughing right out loud at them, but he took a sip of soup instead. "Yum," he said, smacking his lips. The soup was a rich spicy broth filled with beans, carrots and other vegetables. He downed the rest in a couple of gulps. "Delicious soup, Mom. Not as spicy as usual, but really good. Any more left?"

His mom smiled at him. Then she turned to Fred and Barney. "You fellows want any more?"

"Ah, no," Fred said, clearing his throat. "It's very good, really, but one bowl's just fine."

"No, thanks," Barney mumbled. He was looking around, probably for somewhere to dump the rest of his bowl.

Sam was munching on a bun, and taking long drinks of water. He sniffed a loud slurpy sniff and wiped his nose on the back of his hand. He didn't seem to want any soup either so Jacob's mom poured the rest into Jacob's bowl and smiled at him. The candlelight flickered on her curly hair, turning it into a golden halo.

Fred, recovered from the spicy soup, was stroking his beard and expounding away again. Still talking mainly to Barney, he explained how these rain forests were "The Lungs of the World," and that's why we should never complain about the rain. In fact we should be Grateful for it. It was Scrubbing the Air for us, Getting Rid of Pollution.

Right, thought Jacob, staring up at the sagging, wet tent roof. We're just soooo grateful.

"I think we should rinse out our bowls now, then all go to bed," his mom said, yawning. "And pray for sunshine when we reach the Oregon coast tomorrow."

Now Jacob couldn't look directly at his mom. The idea of her sleeping with Fred, curled up beside him in their zipped-together sleeping bags, was just way too embarrassing.

At the beginning of the journey, Fred had suggested that each person should be responsible for his or her own dishes, each a different colour plastic, for the whole trip. Jacob's were red. That was fine with him. He surely didn't want any of *their* germs.

After quickly rinsing out his bowl in a pail of water, he dashed across the campsite through the dark rainy night to his and Minerva's tent, following the light from her flashlight.

"Take your shoes off before you come in," Minerva directed.

"Okay, okay," he said, diving into the tent and pulling off his running shoes. He pushed them under the door flap and peeled off his wet socks.

By the flashlight's dim light, he saw that Minerva had already spread her stuff out on one side of the tent, leaving room for him on the other side. It was a good-sized tent with plenty of room for two kids although the roof sagged under the rain. While Minerva got ready for bed, he piled his stuff on his side and unrolled his sleeping bag on his foam pad. Then he shunted out of his cold wet jeans and jacket and crawled into his sleeping bag in his underwear and T-shirt.

At first he couldn't stop shivering. Everything felt cold and damp. He pulled the top of the sleeping bag close around his neck and wished he'd at least brought a pillow. The ground was as hard as a board and the foam pad didn't help at all. Finally he lay on his back with one arm crooked under his head. He shut his eyes and concentrated on falling asleep but Minerva was grumbling while she fiddled with her CD player.

"Some lousy holiday!" she muttered. "Hey, Jay. How about heading back to Vancouver with me? Bet we could hop a bus."

"What? Go back to Vancouver?" Jacob had to admit the idea had appeal. Any plan to get away from the freaky Finkles was appealing. But then, what would he and Minerva do all summer? Besides, who could they stay with?

"This trip's going to be the pits," Minerva continued. "I just know it. Sitting all day cooped up in that smelly old car. Then camping every night in this mushy tent, listening to those losers argue non-stop for a whole month. I don't know why I ever agreed to come along."

"Mom said we won't be driving the whole time," Jacob

said. "We'll be spending some time in California looking around. We'll get to check out San Francisco and L.A. Disneyland and Hollywood. We'll probably get to tour Universal Studios and see how they made those special effects for *Jurassic Park*. L.A.'s going to be so cool. Then Mexico. I really want to go to Mexico and play some soccer there. So I think I'll stick it out. Anyway, we don't have much choice, do we? I mean, Mom wouldn't let us stay home alone."

Minerva pushed a long curly strand of hair away from her face and stared across the tent at him. The flashlight made her dark eyes look shiny. "I'm sure I could stay at Marty's or with one of my other friends. Couldn't you stay with one of your friends?"

"The only one would be Max and he'll be away at camp most of the summer."

"Mom would never let me take the bus back home alone," Minerva said. "That's for sure. I mean, she should. I *am* fifteen. But I know she just wouldn't."

"Besides, what home?" Jacob said. "We've moved out of the townhouse, remember?"

Less than a week before the wedding, the Armstrongs had moved out of their townhouse. Most of their furniture was now stored in the basement of the Finkle house. Minerva and Jacob were sharing a temporary bedroom in the Finkle's den.

"Right," Minerva grumbled. "I'll sure be glad when Mom and Fred finally find a house big enough for all of us. One thing for sure, I'm not going to stay in anyone's mouldy old basement." Her CD player finally started working. She adjusted the earphones, leaned back to listen to the music and clicked off the flashlight. Now it was pitch dark.

Above the rain dripping on the tent roof, Jacob could hear the tinny vibrations of the Jamaican reggae king from the 1980s, Bob Marley. That's practically all Minerva and her friends listened to these days even though the singer had died years ago. It wasn't bad music, thought Jacob. But to listen to it all the time? Amazing she didn't get sick of it.

The rain was softer now, a gentle swishing sound on the tent. Think of something nice, his mom used to tell him when he was a little kid and couldn't get to sleep. Think of a place you'd like to be.

So he thought about a grassy field somewhere in Mexico. He would be there with a bunch of other guys, kicking his soccer ball back and forth across the field, dancing this way, and that way, avoiding being checked, dribbling the ball right down the field, feinting left, then right, the ball attached to his foot like glue. The sun would be warm on his back. He'd flex his shoulders, feeling the warmth in them, the power. Then with a hard swift kick, wham! Right smack into the net! Impossible to stop! Great corner shot! Gooaalll! He would raise his hands above his head and jog around the field, his Mexican team mates shouting, "*Bravo, Jelé! Bravo!*"

3

The next thing Jacob knew, a sliver of light sky was visible through the mesh window of the tent. Morning! It was still raining though — he noted the dripping trees. The arm under his head was numb. He stretched and wiggled his hand, trying to get the blood circulating. His watch glowed at him: 6:27.

On the other side of the tent, Minerva was snoring deeply. Jacob sat up and reached for his jeans. They were still damp but he slid them on anyway. They felt cold on his legs. Well, he'd warm up soon enough. He pulled his soccer ball out from under his sleeping bag. He would go out and kick it around for a while. What had the Finkle kid said? Practise makes perfect. Right. He jammed on his running shoes, not bothering with socks.

Minerva grunted as she awoke. "Where are you going?" she asked, yawning.

"Nowhere. Just out."

"You'll get soaked.

"So?" he shrugged and headed outside.

Although it was still raining, Jacob dropped his ball and dribbled it between the puddles down the narrow gravel road to the next campsite. It was empty. It looked like they were practically the only ones in the whole camp. Probably everyone else was being sensible and staying in a motel. The road was lined with huge trees, their massive trunks and long branches stretching over thick, bright green undergrowth. Not a good place to lose his ball. He flicked it up on his instep and turned to dribble it back. Someone was coming towards him.

It was his mom, with her raincoat draped over her head. Her skirt clung damply to her legs. "Good morning," she said with a wide smile. "And how did you sleep?"

"Not bad." He couldn't ask her the same thing. This whole honeymoon business was way too embarrassing.

"Fred's making porridge for breakfast. Should be ready soon."

"Porridge? Yuck!"

"Watch your manners now, Jacob. Porridge is a very nourishing breakfast."

He noticed, though, that when they were all crowded in the tent and eating, his mom didn't eat much of hers. The only way he managed to swallow down his share was by sprinkling on a good thick layer of brown sugar. When he finished he went back outside and rinsed his bowl. After he and Minerva had taken down their tent and packed it away, he continued working out with his ball until everyone else was ready to go.

He had time for a good long work-out because it took
the Finkles half the morning to get organized. Sam refused
to get out of bed until his father finally threatened that if
he didn't get a move on, he would dump Sam out of his
sleeping bag, right smack into a puddle.

Sam had finally crawled grumpily out of the tent and
ended up dressing in the car, while Barney had to take
down the wet tent by himself.

"It's just not fair," Barney fumed. "Sam slept in this tent
too."

"If we waited for him to be ready, we'd have to wait until
the cows come home," his dad said.

"Until the cows come home. Hey, I've got to put that
into my act," Barney said, rummaging through his pockets
for his notebook.

"Wait until we're on our way," his dad said. "All aboard
now. Everyone."

Jacob made a beeline for the front seat next to his mom.
Minerva glared at him. "That's my seat."

"Not now, it isn't," he said, grinning in her face.

Their mother said, "Everyone should have a turn sitting in the front, Minerva. You sat here yesterday."

Barney and Sam both claimed the window seats in the
back so Minerva had to sit squashed between them. Now
she was part of a Finkle sandwich. Jacob felt sorry for her,
but not sorry enough to switch places.

He sure was glad he didn't have to sit next to sulky-Sam
this time as they bounced down the rough road away

from their campsite. The kid was all sharp angry elbows and knees as he thrashed around tugging on his clothes. And even worse, his clothes looked filthy and he stunk as bad as a school toilet.

Minerva jammed on her earphones, crossed her arms, and stared straight ahead, glassy-eyed, ignoring everyone while Barney scribbled madly in his joke notebook and Sam stuck out his bottom lip and sulked. It was as if the whole back seat was seething.

As the big hunk of station wagon swayed around the tight bends and bounced through the puddles along the mountain road, Fred and Jacob's mother chatted away cheerfully about politics. Or was it unions? Some boring old thing.

Although Jacob's jeans were still damp, he felt warm and loose after his work-out. He held his ball between his knees. It was damp too and smelled good, of wet moss and ferns. He stretched out his legs and propped his bare feet up on the dashboard. The dripping green forest lurched by the car window. He rested his chin on his ball and thought about kicking it along a wide sandy beach somewhere in Mexico, past one tall white-capped wave, then another, and another, digging his toes into the firm warm sand. There'd be other guys there, the sun glistening on their brown backs and on their wide friendly white smiles.

Mexico. Their destination. Jacob could hardly wait. He hugged his ball on his lap. They played plenty of soccer down there. They must, since soccer was the national sport of Mexico. There was probably a soccer game going on every minute of every day at the local parks, in vacant lots, back lanes, all over the place. That's what his dad had told him a few years ago.

"Every little park, there's a game happening," his dad had said. "That's how it is back home in Jamaica too. The kids, when they're not in school, that's what they do all day. Just play ball. One day, we'll all go down there to Mexico. The whole family together. You'll love it."

On Tuesdays and Thursdays, Jacob's dad would rush home from the high school where he taught Math so he and Jacob could watch World Soccer on TV together. Come to think of it, Jacob's tenth birthday was one of the last days they had spent in their old house on Twenty-fifth Avenue. That day his dad had arrived home late with a crazily wrapped present for him that was more Scotch Tape than paper.

Jacob couldn't believe it when he opened the parcel. From the shape, he could tell it was a ball, and he hoped it was a soccer ball. When he ripped off the paper, he saw it was a soccer ball, all right. But not just any soccer ball. It was a hand-stitched, genuine leather, regulation sized, World Cup Supari!

"Wow! Thanks, Dad!" He'd lunged at his father and hugged him tight. He still remembered the tobacco smell of his dad's rough tweed jacket.

But the good warm feeling hadn't lasted long. Soon his mom and dad were yelling at each other.

"Ah, Len. Why couldn't you at least be on time for the child's birthday?" his mother said.

"Rosa. Get off me back. I'm here now, aren't I?"

The next morning, there had been quite a row. Both Jacob and Minerva had cleared out. He'd gone on a long bike ride down along the beach. By supper time, Minerva was still not back from her friend's house.

A couple of days later everything collapsed. His dad packed up his stuff and left to live in an apartment downtown. Then they all moved: he, Minerva and his mother into a townhouse closer to the high school where his mom was the librarian and where Minerva would attend in the fall. Jacob's mom said they might as well move before school started up again. Jacob decided to stay at his old elementary school so he had to take the bus all the next year.

The soccer ball, though. Jacob inhaled its tangy leather smell. It reminded him of his dad and those good times they used to have together watching sports on TV, a joke never far away. And soccer. His dad knew every single thing there was to know about the NSL, the National Soccer League.

It was soon after they had moved into the townhouse that the terrible accident happened. Jacob still hated thinking about it. His mother had come into his room late one night, her eyes red from crying, to tell him that his father had been killed in a car accident early that morning.

"A truck slammed into the side of his car and he died instantly. He probably didn't suffer, so that's a blessing," she said, wiping tears from her cheeks.

For a long time after, Jacob had felt desolate. There was

this enormous hole in his life. For one thing, he didn't have anyone to talk to about his games. One time when he had scored a fantastic kick from behind the centre line, he didn't bother telling anyone. Minerva wasn't that interested. And if he told his mom, she'd just say, "Oh, that's nice, Sweetie. Did you have a good time?"

As soon as they got to Mexico, he was going to find the games and he'd play and play soccer all day long, from early in the morning until late at night. He knew Mexico wasn't exactly Brazil, the home of Pelé, the most famous soccer player who ever lived, but it was still part of Latin America. He'd learned about it in Social Studies.

After a while, Fred flicked off the windshield wipers. It had finally stopped raining. Mounds of grey clouds drifted by the car window and parted to reveal big lakes of blue sky. They had turned south along the Oregon Coast on Highway 101, the Pacific Coast Highway. It was scenic, all right. The sparkling sea rolled onto long sandy beaches in frothy waves and crashed against high rocky cliffs and weird rocks that stuck straight out of the sand.

"They call those rocks sea stacks and they make this whole coast tortuous for landing boats," Fred said. "And this is Lincoln City," he went on, lecturing in his travel-guide voice. "This is the forty-fifth parallel, which is exactly half-way between the equator and the North Pole. Now isn't that something!"

The sun shone on the top of Jacob's head. He lounged back on the seat and shut his eyes to face the sun's rays. It felt great, warming his forehead and cheeks.

"The famous Oregon Sand Dunes aren't too far," Fred continued. "We could camp there tonight."

"Sand dunes?" Jacob said, sitting up. "Isn't that where they have those awesome dune buggies?"

"A dune buggy ride!" his mother said. "Yes! We must all try that!"

"But Rosa," Fred protested, "dune buggies are probably the most dangerous vehicles in North America, to say nothing of how they pollute the air. With their two-stroke engines, they're as bad as snowmobiles."

"We can't come all this way to the world famous Oregon Dunes and not try out a dune buggy, Fred. We'll be very careful. Don't you worry now, pet." She patted his hand on the steering wheel.

It was a pale hand. Pale and hairy beside Jacob's mother's smooth brown one. And reddish hairs sprouted from Fred's knuckles.

They found a campground south of the small coastal town of Florence. Huge, rolling mounds of sand of the Oregon Dunes stretched out behind their campsite.

The evening was cool and dry with a steady breeze blowing from the sea hidden by the mounds of sand. The sun had dipped below the dunes but the sky was still a light rosy grey. Seagulls wheeled overhead, crying out to each other.

After supper clean-up, Jacob dropped his ball to the sandy road in front of their picnic table and nudged it with his foot away from the campsite.

"Before you leave, Jacob," his mom said. "There's a slide show this evening explaining the history of these dunes. Want to come?"

"No way. I hate those historical slide shows. Way too bor-ring. I'll just kick my ball around for a while." He flicked his ball up and caught it, balancing it on the top of his foot. He kicked it up again and it bounced off his chest and rolled down the sandy road. He sprinted after it.

"Don't think I'll go to that slide show either," Barney said and followed Jacob.

"We'll see you two in an hour or so," his mom called after them. "Don't get into any mischief, now."

Jacob hurried as he dribbled his ball past some other campsites to where the road ended in thick bush. He tried to put some distance between himself and Barney with his barnyard jokes, but Barney kept right behind him.

Jacob grabbed his ball and started climbing a steep sandy mound. He tried sprinting but it was tough to hurry. The faster he tried to go, the more his feet sank into the soft sand. It was like going uphill through heavy, knee-deep water.

When he finally made it to the top of the ridge, he was puffing hard. He looked around. Wow! Rolling sand hills, cut by dark shadows and a few scrubby clumps of shore pine or long sea grass, stretched out as far as he could see. The sand had a pinkish tinge, reflecting the setting sun. A breeze blowing in from the ocean smelled salty and sea-weedy, reminding him of the wide beaches at Spanish Banks in Vancouver where he and his dad used to spend hours, kicking around a soccer ball.

He dropped his ball to the sand and nudged it back and forth, from left foot to right.

Barney soon caught up to him. He was breathing hard too. "Hey, Jay!" Pant, pant. "You heard the one about the cow that …"

Before he could finish the joke, riddle, whatever, Jacob kicked his ball at him. Hard. Anything to avoid another cow joke!

Barney grunted and made a lame attempt to kick the ball back, but his feet got tangled and he tripped. The ball rolled past him down a steep slope and into some bushes.

"Oh, no!" Jacob cried. He dove down the sandy slope after his ball and, tumbling head over heels, crashed into the prickly bushes. He scrambled to his feet and tried to push into the bushes but they grew so thickly that he couldn't.

"Hey, Barney," he yelled over his shoulder. "Come and give me a hand down here, will ya? Can't find my ball." After all, it's all your stupid fault it's lost, he muttered to himself. He found a stick and started whacking at the bushes.

Barney slid down the slope and stood there with his hands in his pockets. He stared at the bushes.

"It's got to be here somewhere," Jacob said. "A ball can't

just disappear into thin air." He couldn't see it at all! It *had* to be here. It just *had* to be.

Barney half-heartedly moved some bushes aside with his foot. He wasn't even trying. Jacob was about to tell him what a loser he was when his stick bashed into something that was not bush. And not sand. He stooped to examine what he'd hit. Shoved under a tangle of twigs was a big black plastic bag.

"Someone's stupid garbage," he muttered, whacking it hard. It split open. Even in the dim light, he could see it wasn't your everyday sort of garbage. Out tumbled a bunch of small packages, wrapped in red tissue paper. He bent to take a closer look.

"Wow!" he squeaked. "Fireworks! A whole pile of fireworks!" He couldn't believe it. Must be a hundred packages. Two hundred! If he'd had these last week at school, he could have sold them and made a bundle! Kids were willing to pay plenty for firecrackers. Since it was illegal for kids in Vancouver to have them, the price skyrocketed.

"Someone must have dumped them," Barney said, looking over his shoulder. "Or maybe stashed them here until the fourth of July. Hey, that's the day after tomorrow, right?"

Jacob nodded. Then an idea occurred to him. "Hey, you want to light off a few?"

"Okay. Man! This is going to be so cool!"

"Just a minute. My ball. I still haven't found my ball."

"It's so dark now, we wouldn't see it if we tripped over it. Come on. Let's get some matches before everyone else comes back from the slide show."

Jacob poked his stick into the bushes one last time. "Guess you're right," he said reluctantly. "I'll come back first thing tomorrow morning."

As he handed Barney a couple of packages of firecrackers, he heard a rustling from on top the knoll. His heart lurched, then beat madly against his ribs. Had the owner of the fireworks returned? He ducked into the bushes and glanced at Barney. He was hiding behind a bush as well, his arm over his head.

Jacob held his breath and listened. It was amazingly quiet now. Far away, someone's radio was playing pop music. That was it. No other sound. Even the seagulls were quiet. Maybe it was just the wind he had heard. He stood up cautiously and reached into the garbage bag for another handful of firecrackers. He stowed them under his T-shirt. Barney grabbed a few more too. Then they scrambled through the bush and were about to start back up the slope when a figure, crouching in the long shadows on the hill, caught Jacob's eye. He was thinking about dropping his loot and making a run for it, when Barney hissed, "Sam! What are you doing here?"

"Oh, Barney. It's just you!" Sam clumped down the slope. "What'd you guys find?" he asked, pointing to Barney's bulging shirt.

"None of your beeswax," Barney snapped, nudging up his glasses. A package of firecrackers slipped out to the ground.

Sam pounced on it. "Wow! Firecrackers! Where'd you guys get these?"

"We found them. Why don't you get lost, Squirt?"

"But where'd you find them? Lucky! There any more?" Sam was about to plunge into the bushes.

"We've already got plenty," Jacob said, handing Sam a couple of packages. "Now let's grab those matches before my mom and your dad come back."

Barney nodded. Jacob and Sam followed him back up the slope and down the other side to the road. They jogged back toward their campsite.

Although it was getting dark, Jacob could see Big Blue from a distance. It glowed almost fluorescently in the twilight. When they got to it, they tried the doors.

"Darn!" Jacob said. "Big Blue's locked up. Now how are we going to get those matches?" He glanced up the road.

"No sign yet of my dad or your mom," Barney said. "But we'll have to act fast."

"I know where some matches are," Sam piped up.

"Where?" Barney asked.

"In the cooking stuff with the stove. I saw Dad put some there."

"So where's the stove?"

"Must be under the table with the rest of the cooking stuff," Jacob said.

It didn't take long to locate the stove and the small metal container of wooden matches. Jacob shook out six. Not too many to be missed, he hoped. He gave two to

Barney but he hesitated before giving any to Sam. "Think he's old enough to handle matches?" he asked Barney.

"Sure I am," Sam said, standing on his toes. "I'm nine, almost. And going to grade four."

"It'll be okay, I guess," Barney said. "We could watch him. You have to promise not to tell though, Sam. You can't tell one single person. Especially not Dad."

"Why not?"

"He'd take them away from us. And the firecrackers too."

"Okay. I won't tell," Sam promised solemnly.

Jacob ripped the red tissue paper off one of his packages. There were about twenty firecrackers the size of his little finger, all lined up, their white string fuses in a tangle.

"Boy, oh boy! This is going to be so cool!" Barney said, jumping around him, pushing up his glasses.

Jacob licked his lips and started untangling the fuses. Then he noticed some people walking down the road towards them.

"They're coming back! We've got to stash these away!" he hissed. They dove for their tents.

As he was hiding the firecrackers under his sleeping bag, he heard Barney mutter to Sam in their tent, "Here. Stash them in here. And remember, don't tell anyone."

"I won't," Sam said. "I already said I wouldn't."

"Yoo-hoo! Anyone here?" Jacob's mom called. "Thought I heard someone."

"Oh, hi," Jacob said, coming out of the tent. Barney emerged from his tent as well. Empty handed, Jacob noted.

When Sam crawled out of the tent he stood in front of it with his hands behind his back, grinning. Guilty-looking nerd, thought Jacob.

"So how was the slide show?" he asked. Not that he wanted to know, but he had to do something to divert attention from Sam.

"Most informative," Fred started in his professor voice. "You boys missed an excellent presentation. Did you know that these sand dunes were created thousands of years ago and they're still being formed today?"

"Really?" Jacob said, nodding and stroking his chin. "Still being formed today. Well, well. How very interesting."

His mother looked at him crossly. She had caught on that he wasn't in the least interested in the formation of the Oregon sand dunes. She untangled herself from Fred's arm around her waist, and said, "You boys want a warm drink before bed? How about a cup of cocoa tea?"

"Yes, please," Jacob said.

"What's cocoa tea?" Barney asked, suspiciously.

"It's really good," Jacob said. "Sort of like hot chocolate. You'll like it. Mom makes it for us all the time in the winter." He held his breath when Fred reached for the stove under the table. Would he notice the missing matches? "So, Fred," he said, to continue distracting him. "Tell us more about these wonderful Oregon dunes. Like, where did all this sand come from?"

Fred smiled at him while he pumped up the camp stove. "Well, it comes from a special type of rocky cliff that used to be here. The winds and waves beat against the cliffs, eroding it until it formed all this sand, then it was deposited on the beach, forming these dunes. As I said, you fellows should have come to the slide show. The ranger had some very impressive slides." He lit the stove without noticing the missing matches.

"Da-ad," Sam piped up. "Can we have a campfire tonight? Can we? Do you got enough matches?"

Jacob's breath caught in his throat. What a jerk! Was the kid about to squeal?

"Boy, sure am bushed," Barney said, yawning. "Hey, that reminds me. Have you guys heard the one about why some cows lie on their backs in the bushes with their legs sticking straight up?"

"Hey, I haven't heard that one," Jacob said with fake enthusiasm. "Why?"

"So they can catch low-flying bush-birds," Barney said.

"Bush-birds?" Sam asked. "What are bush-birds?"

"Birds that live in bushes, of course," Barney said.

Jacob grinned with relief. Barney's terrible joke had managed to distract not only Sam, but hopefully Fred as well.

Fred said, "It's too late to start messing around with a campfire tonight. Time we all got ready for bed."

"Right. Tomorrow is dune buggy day," Jacob's mom said, handing around the warm drinks.

Jacob took a sip of the sweet, spicy chocolate drink.

It slid down his throat and landed comfortably in his stomach. "Yum," he murmured.

Barney sipped his drink cautiously, nodded and slurped down the rest.

"We shall see about dune buggies tomorrow," Fred said. "We shall see."

Jacob stared across the picnic table at Fred. Is this how this whole trip was going to be? Was Fred going to veto every single thing that was the least bit fun?

4

After rinsing his cup and brushing his teeth, Jacob ducked into his tent. He wanted to check that the firecrackers were well hidden under his jacket before his sister came in. He didn't think she'd squeal, but he had to be on the safe side.

"Jacob," his mother said from the tent entrance. "You all set for bed?"

He quickly shoved his jacket on top of the firecrackers. "Just about," he told her.

"Good night, then. Sleep well."

"Good night, Mom."

He wormed into his sleeping bag and curled up with his head on his jacket. Was it obvious the firecrackers were stashed there?

Minerva crawled into the tent soon after.

"Where were you?" he asked.

For once she wasn't plugged into her stereo. "That slide show was so-o-o boring," she whispered, wriggling into her sleeping bag. "So I took off and went for a walk into the dunes. Tried to get out to the sea but the going got too hard. What did you guys do?"

"Not much. Kicked the ball around a bit."

Jacob thought about his ball with deep longing. He'd go back in the morning as soon as it was light enough. He'd be sure to find it then. He *had* to.

"My ball rolled down into a bush in the dunes and it was too dark to find it. I'll get it in the morning. Man, it gets dark so fast around here."

"I noticed that too. Probably because we're a lot farther south or something. I guess you don't remember, but back home in Jamaica they don't ever have twilight. As soon as the sun sets, that's it. Total darkness, as if someone pulled a light switch. It's something to do with being so close to the equator or something."

"Strange," Jacob said drowsily. He didn't remember anything at all about Jamaica. But then, he wasn't even three when his family moved to Canada. One day he was going back there to check it out. But for now, Mexico would have to do.

The next morning, Jacob woke early. It was barely light. The ground under his back was hard and lumpy. He slithered out of his sleeping bag, and pulled on his jeans and running shoes. Then he slipped out of the tent.

A bird in a tree just above his head trilled good morning. Another bird a few trees away answered. Then it was quiet.

Everyone but those early birds must still be asleep.

He jogged down the road between the campsites to the steep trail that led up into the dunes. He climbed the trail, sinking to his knees into the loose sand. Once he got to the top of the dunes, he looked around. It was lighter up here above the trees. The sky to the east was tinged pink but it was still dark grey in the west toward the sea. He couldn't see the water, but he knew it must be somewhere under those dark clouds. The morning breeze was cool against his cheeks. He shivered and pulled his shirt closer around his back.

It was near here that he'd kicked his ball the night before. He didn't know where exactly. Barney was standing over there by the path, he remembered, and Jacob had kicked the ball at him. If Barney hadn't been such a klutz, he would have blocked the ball and kicked it back like any normal kid.

Jacob nudged a round stone and it rolled down a dip. He loped down the slope after it, taking giant strides until he came to the thick bushes. He started bashing them with a stick. What was that round lump under the bush back there? Just the garbage bag of firecrackers they'd found the night before. Should he help himself to a few more? No. Maybe not. They already had plenty.

He whacked and whacked at the bushes some more, growing more and more desperate. What if his ball was really lost? What if he never saw it again? Ever! It was the only thing he had from his father. He couldn't lose it. It must be in here somewhere. It must!

He whacked some more, harder now, pushing deeper into the bushes. The back of his neck became prickly with sweat. He just had to find it! He started panting. His stick whacked against something that wasn't a log. What was it? He held his breath and peered closer. Yes! It was his ball! It had rolled into a shallow hole beside a stunted tree. He grabbed it and hugged it tightly. Relief! If he'd lost it ... No, he couldn't bear to think about that.

As he emerged from the bushes, he heard the sound of a buzzing motor. Awfully early for a dune buggy to be streaking across the dunes, he thought. As the buzz became a roar, his first instinct was to dive back into the bushes. But why should he hide? He hadn't done anything wrong.

A sleek lime-green dune buggy buzzed down the slope and squealed to a stop beside the bush. The buggy was a low two-seater job with enormous knobby tires. A couple of scruffy teenagers sprang out and headed past Jacob into the bushes without saying hello. Must be the guys who'd hidden the bag of firecrackers. He didn't wait around to find out. He took off up the sandy dune, his feet whirling like a windmill. He scrambled up over the ridge and down the other side to the road. He didn't stop running until he was back at his campsite, number 382. He leaned against the big old station wagon panting like mad, trying to catch his breath. The green dune buggy sped by. Before he could duck out of sight, it screeched to a stop and backed up. The driver raised his goggles and took a long mean look at him. Then he revved up the motor and sped away.

Jacob gulped hard and dropped his ball to the ground. He kicked it against a broad tree trunk and it bounced back. He kicked it again. And again. He got it right on the edge of his foot most of the time. As he got the rhythm up, he began to feel calmer. His breath came back. He pulled his breath deep into his chest and his rib cage expanded as he filled his lungs with cool morning sea air. He had to be careful not to kick the ball too hard. He didn't want to lose it again. Man, it felt good just nipping it with the edge of his foot. Nip, nip, nip.

After breakfast Fred pulled his socks up and adjusted the garters around his knobby knees. "So how about a hike to explore the dunes?" he said.

"Maybe we'll find a dune buggy to rent up there," Jacob's mom said.

"Yes!" Barney shouted. "That would be the best!"

"We shall see," Fred said. "We shall see."

They filed down the road to another path that led uphill through some scrubby woods to the dunes. As usual, Barney and Sam competed for their father's attention, one on either side of him, bouncing along, each trying to out-talk the other. Barney usually won, but sometimes Fred said, "One moment, Barnaby. Give Sam a chance now."

Jacob's mother walked behind them and Jacob and Minerva pulled up the rear, passing the soccer ball back and forth across the path in time with the reggae tune blaring from Minerva's boom box. Jacob trusted her not to miss a pass and lose the ball. Even fiddling with her boom box, you could count on her to play an excellent game of soccer.

They emerged from the shady woods and were confronted by a bright blue sky over the rolling dunes.

"Wow!" Jacob said, picking up his ball. "Take a look at that!" In the bright sunlight, the dunes looked even bigger than they had that morning. They were like a giant's sand castle with steep slopes of sand descending into ravines. "This must be what the Sahara Desert looks like."

Minerva nodded and kicked off her running shoes. She tied the laces together, slung them over her shoulder and started walking along the narrow sandy ridge with her arms outstretched, like a tightrope walker.

They all shucked off their shoes. The warm sand folded around Jacob's bare feet like cocoons. He kicked at it and sauntered along the firmer sand on the ridge, following Minerva, plunging down one dune, then trudging up another. A sea breeze blew past his ears. When he reached the top of a ridge, he looked down into a hollow where a pond reflected trees and bushes and blue sky. They had found an oasis in the sand dune desert.

"Now that's the place for me," Jacob's mother panted when she made it to the top of the ridge. She bounded down the slope towards the pond, her full skirt billowing like a flowered sail.

They all bounced down after her. Jacob splashed into the pond after Barney. The water was surprisingly cool in the bright sun.

"Oh, my! Now, this is the life!" his mother sighed. She sat by the water's edge, stretched out her shiny brown legs, and closed her eyes.

Fred sat behind her and stroked her back affectionately. She leaned back and smiled up at him.

Jacob's stomach churned. Why did they have to smooch like that in public? It's true they were on their honeymoon. Still ...

Barney splashed out of the water, plunked himself down beside them and opened his joke book. "Here's one for you, Dad," he said. "What would you call a cow at the north pole?"

Fred shook his head. "Don't know that one." He continued to stroke Jacob's mom's back.

"I'd call it one very lost cow," Barney said.

"Right," Fred said absently. "That's a good one."

Sam nudged into his other side. "Da-ad," he said. "Why is all this sand here? Where'd it come from? Why is the water so cold when the sun's so hot?"

Fred patiently answered each question, but Jacob knew Sam wasn't listening because he started asking the same questions over again.

Meanwhile, Barney interrupted with another one of his jokes. "Did you hear what happened when a herd of wild bulls ran through the cows' milking shed?"

"No, what?" his dad muttered.

"It was udder chaos. Get it? Udder chaos. You know, a cow's udders?"

"Right, right, right," Fred said.

Minerva left her boom box beside her mother and climbed back up the sand dune. Jacob followed her. When they reached the top, he heard Fred say, "Why don't you two go up there with Jacob and Minerva? Don't you want to explore a bit?"

"Oh, no!" Jacob groaned. "Here come the barnyard jokes again."

Minerva snickered.

"Well, okay," Barney said. "Hey, you guys," he called after them. "You ever heard the one about what happened when a bunch of wild bulls ran through the milking shed?"

"It was udder chaos," Jacob muttered.

"That's a great one, don't you think?" Barney said. "Get it? Udder? Udder chaos? You know. Cow's udders. Wonder if I should use it before or after the story about the guy who got lost."

Jacob grunted and nudged his ball away. It rolled down the other side of the ridge. "My ball!" he yelled. He galloped after it as it rolled out of sight. Not again! Anything to get away from those barnyard jokes.

Barney bounded down on Jacob's heels and Minerva followed.

The ball had rolled to a stop at the bottom of the hill behind a small bush. When Jacob caught it up in his arms, he felt like shaking his finger at it and saying, "Naughty, naughty."

Before Barney could start with the jokes again, Minerva said, "Here. Pass."

As Jacob nudged his ball gently in her direction, he heard the sound of a motor coming toward them. A lime-green dune buggy flipped over a mound and headed straight for them. Jacob caught his breath. Was it the teenagers he'd seen earlier that morning? He thought it was the same dune buggy but he couldn't be sure. Maybe they'd tracked him down and even found the missing firecrackers in his tent. Maybe they were coming to nab him. Jacob grabbed his ball and held his breath.

But it was just one guy. When the dune buggy came down the slope and whizzed around them a couple of times, Jacob saw the driver wasn't either of the teenagers. He looked older, more clean-cut. He shouted over the sound of the motor. "Where's your dad?"

"Here I am." Fred came puffing up the other side of the ridge.

"Man! Riding that would be the ultimate fun experience," breathed Barney.

Minerva nodded, agreeing.

"Not many people out in the dunes yet this morning," the driver said when Fred reached them. "You the people who told the camp manager you're looking to rent a vehicle?"

"Right-o. That would be us."

"You could rent this one but I'd have to drive it. The dune

police are mighty strict about who drives these things."

"But I'm an engineer," Fred protested. "I'd want to be sure it'll be safe."

"Sorry. Them's the rules."

"I'm sure it'll be fine," Jacob's mother said. She had climbed the ridge to join them as well. "This young man looks like an experienced driver."

"How much do you charge?" Fred asked.

"Twenty dollars an hour."

"Twenty American dollars? That's outrageous!"

"Now, Fred. It's not so much, really. And the young man would have to pay for his gas and everything," Jacob's mother said, patting Fred's arm.

"Maybe you're right, Rosa."

"Can I go first?" Barney begged, bouncing around the buggy. "Can I? Can I?"

Fred did a quick check of the buggy. "Roll bar, seat belts, crash helmets. Looks safe enough, I guess," he said, nodding at Barney.

"Yippee!" Barney yelled. Soon he was securely installed in the passenger seat, buckled in, goggled and helmeted.

Then, in a spray of sand, the dune buggy took off, up over the ridge, down and around. When Barney came back, his freckled cheeks were red and he was grinning.

"That was the best," he said. "The very best!"

Sam had a turn and so did Minerva. When Jacob's mother roared off, her wide skirt flapped out behind the buggy.

As he waited his turn, Jacob wasn't sure if he wanted to go. Maybe the driver was a friend of the teenagers from this morning and they had found out somehow that he was the one who had taken some of their firecrackers. Maybe he'd flip Jacob over for revenge. Or maybe push him down some steep cliff. Jacob sat at the top of the ridge hugging his ball. It seemed to him that his mother had been gone a long time. When she finally returned, her face was glowing with excitement.

"Come now, Jacob," she said. "It's your turn. It's wonderful. So invigorating."

So Jacob reluctantly handed his ball to Minerva and soon found himself in the bucket seat. It was so low that he was almost sitting on the ground. He stretched his legs straight out to the foot rests and buckled on a wide shoulder strap that held him firmly against the seat. He adjusted the goggles and the helmet. Then he nodded that he was ready.

The motor roared and off they sped. Jacob felt as if he'd left his insides behind. He kept his mouth tightly shut so he wouldn't get a mouthful of sand. They lurched over a ridge, and plunged straight down a steep sandy cliff, then straight up again, around and around. He lost all sense of direction. A blur of sand mounds flashed by. The buggy went over and around until Jacob was dizzy and his head buzzed with the whine of the motor. Down in a deep trench, it came to a sudden stop.

The driver flipped up his goggles and stared at Jacob with hard blue eyes. "Look, kid. Some of our stuff's missing."

"What stuff? We didn't ..." Jacob protested. So they did know he and Barney had taken some of the firecrackers. And this guy *was* connected to the scruffy pair this morning. How had he tracked Jacob down?

"I'm just warning you," the guy said. "You rat on us, and you'll be sorry. You're real easy to trace. We got your license number. Understand, kid?"

Jacob gulped hard and nodded. He'd never met such a mean looking guy in his whole entire life. Those icy blue eyes gave him the creeps all the way down to his toes. Finally the guy put his goggles back on, revved up the motor, and they took off. Soon they were back where they'd started.

Fred had his camera out and was busily snapping pictures, so Jacob had to look cool and force his stiff lips into a smile although his heart was pounding so hard, he had trouble breathing.

"Can I have another go, Dad? Can I? Please, please," Barney begged. "It's way better than a roller coaster any day."

The driver said, "Sorry, but I've got to be shoving off now." After Fred gave him some money, he gunned the motor and roared off in a cloud of sand.

Then Jacob had a jumping fit. He sped along the ridge, leapt over the edge of the cliff, high into the air, and plunged down to the soft sand below. Minerva leapt after him and landed even farther out.

As Jacob scrambled up the cliff again, Barney jumped over and so did Sam, shouting, "Look out below!"

Jacob leapt out from the ridge again and again and again. Oh, the glorious freedom of sailing though the air, knowing it was soft sand below.

"How about all lining up for an action shot?" Fred said. "You too, Rosa."

So they all lined up at the top of the ridge. Fred pointed his camera at them. "All together now. One, two, three, jump!"

Jacob put everything into his leap. He used all his fears and anger to push himself out, far over the cliff, sending his legs up and out.

As he sailed from the high ridge, way out and down the slope, the tension inside his stomach stretched like an elastic band. It stretched and stretched. The soft sand rose to cushion him. He landed and the tension gushed away.

That time he jumped even farther than Minerva did.

5

On the way back to their campsite, Barney caught up with Jacob. "Want to light off those firecrackers tonight?" he whispered.

"Sure. I guess. After supper. When it's really dark. They'll probably go for a walk again. If it gets as dark as last night, no one will guess that it's us making all the racket."

That night they had a late supper. It was Fred's turn to cook. When the macaroni and cheese finally arrived, it was so mushy that it dissolved in Jacob's mouth without him even chewing. But he was so hungry, he slurped up his share and looked around for more. Barney beat him to the pot and volunteered to clean it so he could scrape out the cheesy bottom.

Sam, under his dad's direction, lit a campfire in the fire pit beside the picnic table. They toasted marshmallows and made sandwiches with the melted marshmallows and pieces of chocolate between two graham crackers. The treat was called "s'mores" because you always wanted some more, Minerva explained.

"Mmmm. Bloomin' delicious," Fred said, wiping some melted marshmallow off his moustache. "We never had anything like this in England."

Beside him, Sam yawned mightily and rubbed his eyes.

"Think you should go to bed now, Sam, before you fall head-first into the fire."

"But, Da-ad," Sam protested.

"Remember the tough time you had getting up this morning? And yesterday? So off to bed with you now."

Sam slowly, reluctantly plodded away, dragging his feet in the sand.

"Such a beautiful night," Jacob's mom sighed, gazing up at the navy blue, star-studded sky. "Anyone for an evening stroll around the camp?"

"Sure," Minerva said.

"I'll come, too," Fred said. "What about you boys?"

"No, thanks," Jacob said.

"I'm kind of tired. Think I'll hit the sack too," Barney yawned. He wiggled his eyebrows above the frames of his glasses at Jacob. Jacob knew what Barney was thinking. Firecrackers!

"Yeah. Me too," Jacob said.

They both wandered to their tents. Jacob ducked inside. He searched under his sleeping bag for the firecrackers. Yes! They were still there.

He heard Sam's voice asking Barney what he was doing.

"Nothing," Barney hissed. "Just checking these firecrackers."

"You and Jacob gonna let them off tonight?"

"Maybe."

"Can I come too?"

"Maybe. Just be quiet, will ya'? We don't want Dad and Rosa to find out."

Jacob left his tent with his toothbrush and went to the tap on the other side of the campsite. He started brushing his teeth and Barney soon joined him with his toothbrush.

"Got them?" Barney asked through the toothpaste foam dripping down his chin.

"Not yet. We'd better wait until our parents are gone."

Barney nodded. As Jacob brushed his teeth, he watched his mom stroll away down the road with Fred on one side and Minerva on the other.

Jacob rinsed out his mouth and whispered, "We could go up into the dunes to let them off. No one will be up there."

"Okay. Sam wants to come."

Jacob shook his head. "He's too young, isn't he?"

"He'll be okay. We'll watch him. He wouldn't want to be left here alone."

Jacob shrugged, so Barney went to get Sam. Jacob ducked back into his tent and stuffed his firecrackers into his jeans pockets along with his matches. When he met Barney and Sam outside, Sam looked so small there beside Barney that Jacob hesitated.

"You got your matches?" Barney whispered.

"Yeah," Jacob said.

"Let's get going before the folks come back."

Barney probably knew his brother better that he did, Jacob decided, so he nodded and led them up the road.

His eyes soon got used to the dark and the night didn't seem as black. There was no moon yet, but the stars were so bright it was easy to believe they were really faraway suns. You never saw stars that bright in the city.

They jogged past the other campsites, which seemed deserted or with occupants who were already in bed. When they reached the sandy cliff, they climbed the steep path toward the ridge.

"Hurry up," Barney nagged.

"I am," Sam said, panting up the slope behind them.

When they were up on the ridge, Jacob looked around. All was quiet and there wasn't a soul in sight. He slid a stash of firecrackers out of his pocket and shook the fuses loose.

"Okay. Here goes!" He struck one of his matches on a stone and touched a fuse. The fuse spat and fizzled in the dark. He flung the firecracker down the cliff into the dark bushes. It exploded, ripping into the night's silence. His stomach lurched and his heart beat like crazy. "Wooie!" he squealed and quickly let off two more with his first match before the match singed his fingertips. The firecrackers exploded in two loud bursts. His ears rang and acrid smoke stung his nostrils.

"That's so cool!" Barney crowed. His grin flashed white as he lit his firecrackers. He flung them down the slope where they exploded in the night air with satisfyingly loud bangs. He got four more lit, two with each match. Then he gave one of his firecrackers to Sam and lit it for him.

Breathing hard with excitement, Sam held onto the firecracker.

"Quick! Throw it out before it explodes in your hand," Jacob told him.

Sam threw it hard. When it exploded, he squealed with delight.

Jacob had only one match left. He decided to let off a whole package with it. He lit the fuses and tossed the whole package down the cliff. "Let's clear out!" he yelled. "It's going to really blast!"

They hurried along the ridge a few meters and ducked into a hollow. The fuses sparked and fizzled. Then the firecrackers exploded. Bang, bang, bang! The racket was fantastic! The bursting firecrackers blasted bright orange flares into the darkness.

"Yippee!" Sam yelled, jumping around.

"Now that should wake up a few people," Jacob laughed. His voice was hoarse with excitement. He inhaled the exciting odour of the exploding firecrackers.

Barney grinned back. They all leaped down the cliff and started back along the road toward their campsite.

Two large figures appeared out of the gloom and barred their way.

Jacob gasped and stepped back.

One of the figures was a tall man with his hands on his hips. The other was shorter, broader. He crossed his arms in front of a large burly chest. "Just a minute, young fellows," he growled. "We want to ask you a few questions."

Jacob saw their hats. Police officers! "Oh, no!" he gasped. His breath caught in his throat and his stomach flipped and knotted.

"You boys know that firecrackers are against the law for minors in this state?" the tall police officer said, pointing a flashlight into their faces.

"And they are definitely banned in the park," the other one growled.

Jacob's tongue went numb. What could he say? He put up an arm to shield his eyes from the dazzling light and shook his head. Barney shook his head too and Sam ducked behind his brother, his eyes scared.

"Where you guys from?" the tall officer asked. His flashlight remained on Jacob.

"British Columbia," he mumbled.

"Where in B.C?"

Jacob told them their address. Barney didn't say anything. He gnawed on his fingernails and fiddled with his glasses, pushing them up onto his nose. They kept sliding back down.

"So where did you fellows get the fireworks? Do they sell them to minors up in Canada?"

"No. We found them in the bush over the other side of that dune," Jacob pointed with his chin.

"There any more left?"

Jacob started to shake his head but Barney piped up, "Sure. A whole garbage bag full. We only took a few."

"Not now there aren't," Jacob said. "I think they came and took them."

"Who? Who took them?"

"I don't know who they were. Just some guys this morning in a dune buggy."

"What are you talking about?" Barney hissed at Jacob. "I don't remember anyone. Were you up before me this morning?"

Jacob shrugged his shoulders at Barney.

The police officers didn't seem to notice Barney; they were concentrating on Jacob. "So what kind of buggy? Do you remember anything about it? Model? Colour?"

"Don't know," Jacob shrugged, digging into the sand with his toes. "Green," he mumbled. "Maybe it was green."

"Okay, fellows," the taller police officer said, jotting down information about them in a notebook. "We won't charge you this time, but we've got your names and address and if you're in possession of any more fireworks you are liable to a five-hundred-dollar fine. Now do you have any more?"

"A few." Jacob pulled out the last package of firecrackers from his pocket and handed it to the police officer. Barney did so as well. He nudged Sam. Sam reluctantly gave up two packages from inside his shirt.

"And that's it? No more? You sure?"

The boys nodded.

"Now we'll take you boys back to your campsite."

"It's okay," Jacob said. "We can find our way."

But as they turned to go down the road, there were two figures walking toward them. Jacob's mother and Fred!

"What's happening?" she said, her voice tight with worry.

"What trouble is this?"

"You the mother?" one of the police officers asked, pointing his flashlight in her direction.

"I certainly am," she said, flinching in the bright light.

"These young fellows were letting off firecrackers in the dunes," the officer informed her.

Jacob's mother's eyes widened angrily as she stared at Jacob. He ducked his head.

"What!" Fred said. "Firecrackers? Our boys? Where on earth did they get them?"

"Said they found them in the woods back there."

"We did," Barney said. "They were just stuffed in an old garbage bag. We didn't know they were illegal."

Jacob couldn't bear to look at his mom. Maybe taking those firecrackers had been really dumb. But he hadn't expected it to be such a big deal. Kids let off firecrackers all the time, especially on Halloween. What if they'd been arrested and fined a whole lot of money? Five hundred bucks! American! It would take years of allowances to cover that.

Fred turned to the police. "Thank you for bringing our boys back," he said. "We'll deal with them now."

When they got back to the campsite, Fred turned on the boys angrily. "I'm surprised at you two!" he said to Barney and Jacob. "You're both old enough to know better. And to involve an eight-year-old in your pranks. That's extremely dangerous and irresponsible."

Jacob's ears burned. He looked down at his feet and shuffled in the dust.

"Sorry," Barney mumbled, kicking at the car's tire.

"It was just a bunch of firecrackers," Jacob shrugged. "What's the big deal?"

"Jacob," his mother warned. "You watch your manners now, child."

"But Mom. We light off firecrackers in Vancouver at Halloween all the time. It's no big deal. We didn't even know they were illegal here in the States."

"The point is," Fred continued, "first, you took something that didn't belong to you. And second, you two involved a younger child in what could have been a very dangerous activity."

Jacob shrugged again. "We couldn't leave such a little kid alone in the campsite. We were looking after him. Anyway, he begged us to let him come along. It wasn't our idea that he come with us. Right, Sam? You tell your dad."

Sam nodded. "It's true, Dad. I wanted to go with them."

Fred looked at Jacob and shook his head. Jacob thought he saw the shadow of a smile cross Fred's lips behind his beard. "Just don't let it happen again."

"Don't worry. It won't," Jacob said. "A fine of five hundred smackeroos! Man oh man! Just think what we could do with all that dough! Right, Barney?"

Barney grinned at him. "You sure know how to talk your way out of trouble. Ever consider a career as a stand-up comic?"

"I could never do that," Jacob said. "I'm allergic to cow jokes."

6

The next morning Big Blue left the Oregon dunes early and headed south for San Francisco. According to the camper's guide, the closest campground to the "Golden Gate City" was a KOA about thirty miles north on the outskirts of the town of Ukiah. When Fred and Jacob's mom checked out the campground, they noted that there was a games room and a swimming pool. So Jacob thought it would probably be okay. There might even be a good field for kicking around his soccer ball. Also, it was far enough away from the Oregon Dunes that the steely-eyed guy and his pals would never find him again. He hoped.

When they reached the campground in mid-morning, they unloaded the camping equipment from the storage box on top of the station wagon and carried the tents out to the grassy field.

"Whoops. Watch your step," Minerva told Jacob as she stepped over a cow pie.

"Looks like this was a cow pasture not so long ago," Jacob said.

Close by, a bunch of cows were lined up behind a new barbed wire fence, calmly staring at them with long-lashed brown eyes, their mouths forever chewing and their long tails swishing back and forth.

"Wow! Just look at all those beautiful cows!" Barney said. "They're the real thing." He stood there with his hands on his hips and stared back at them.

Jacob snorted. If Barney had a tail, he would probably swish it back and forth too.

"You all know what a cow is," Barney said.

Jacob moaned. Here we go again.

"It's a non-stop cud-chewing machine. What about this one," Barney said, consulting his notebook. "How do you catch a cow?"

"Why would you want to?" Jacob asked, shaking the tent out of the bag and looking around for a clean flat place to set it up.

"You hide in the bushes and yell, 'Free hay! Free hay!' Get it?"

"Yeah, sure. Very funny."

After they had pitched their tents, they all piled back into the car and headed south for San Francisco. This time, Jacob got to sit in front beside the window. His mother was at the wheel and Fred sat between them, rattling the maps and nervously chewing the edge of his moustache. Heavy traffic was crawling along the interstate highway, four lanes heading into the city and four lanes coming out.

"Change lanes, Rosa," Fred directed. "The left lane's much faster."

"Is anyone coming? I can't see. We didn't adjust the rear-view mirrors. Could you look for me, please, Minerva?"

Minerva was sitting in the back seat directly behind her mother, but she was plugged into her stereo and didn't hear the question.

"Minerva!" her mother shouted. "Can we go? Is it safe to switch lanes now?"

The car lurched off the road while Jacob's mom strained to see out the mirror. Jacob braced himself against the door, expecting to crash into the ditch at any second.

"Blimey! I can't see either," Fred said, gripping the back of the seat and peering around. "There's so bloomin' much stuff back there that it's blocking the mirror." He reached back and tapped Minerva's knee. "Minny!" he said. "Would you please check if the left lane is free so we can change lanes?"

Minerva pulled off her earphones. "Don't call me Minny," she said, scowling at him. "My name's Minerva."

"Sorry, I forgot," he apologized. "Your mother told me how you hate that name. Now could you please look and see if we can change lanes?"

Minerva rolled down her window. The wind caught her hair and whipped it around her face. "Not yet," she shouted. "After this red car. Okay, Mom. Now! Go now!"

Big Blue lurched into the next lane, pressing Jacob hard against Fred.

But that lane ended up being just as slow. Rush hour

traffic was still heading into San Francisco at eleven o'clock in the morning.

Jacob's mother swung the steering wheel right and left and right again and the car wove between the slow moving vehicles on the overpasses. Every time they changed lanes, it was a great production. Jacob had to check the traffic when they wanted the right lane and Minerva checked for the left lane.

"Let's have some music at least," their mother said, wiping her sweaty forehead with a tissue. "How about playing us one of your good reggae CDs, Minerva?"

Minerva put a CD into her boom box and turned it on good and loud. When the music erupted from the back seat, Fred grimaced. But Jacob and his mom loved it.

"I shot de sheriff …" Jacob's mom sang along with the Jamaican music, tapping the steering wheel like a drum. The car swayed to and fro down the highway in time with the music like a large woman dancing across a crowded dance floor.

Fred gripped the dashboard as if he expected a crash at any moment. When the song was finally over, he cleared his throat and said, "Um, perhaps we should listen to our Spanish tape now so we'll know some Spanish when we get to Mexico."

He fumbled through the glove compartment and found a Spanish tape which he slid it into the car tape deck.

"*Uno, dos, tres, cuatro*." The tape started with numbers, first in Spanish, then in English.

Mexico. Jacob hugged his soccer ball on his knee. "How do you say, 'Where's the game?' in Spanish?" he asked his mother.

"I don't know," she said. "Do you, Fred?"

"Um, I think it goes something like this: '*¿Dónde está el juego?*'"

Jacob repeated the Spanish words a few times. "Thanks. I've got it now."

"You're going to use that when we get to Mexico?"

"Maybe."

As they approached the city, the traffic got even thicker so the car slowed to a crawl.

"*¿Dónde está el juego?*" Jacob whispered to himself, getting his lips around the unfamiliar sounds.

He could picture the whole thing. The sun would be shining in a little Mexican village. In a vacant lot, six or eight guys would be kicking around an old bundle of rags. That's what he'd read that Pelé had used when he was growing up and couldn't find a ball.

Jacob would arrive at the game with his ball under his arm and all the guys would crowd around him and beg him to play. In a few minutes they'd divide into two teams and he'd show them a few neat moves he'd been practising. And he'd learn a few new moves from them. They'd play all day, whipping up and down the field. The guys would be astonished at his marvelous goals.

As the sun began to set, they'd all be grinning at him, and thanking him for the game. "*Gracias, gracias.*" They'd plan to meet again the next day.

Man! It was going to be fantastic when they got to Mexico!

"San Francisco. Home of Lombard Street, the crookedest street in the world," Jacob's mother announced from behind the steering wheel. She slowed the car and they all peered up the steepest, crookedest and narrowest city street Jacob had ever seen. A continuous stream of tourist-filled cars wound back and forth, down the narrow street, which was hemmed in by fancy apartments and large planters overflowing with colourful flowers.

"The reason they made it so crooked is because it's so steep," Fred explained. "You know how you weave back and forth up a steep hill with your bike? That's what they did here. Went back and forth to get up the hill. That's why it's so twisty."

"It's very pretty," Jacob's mother said. "But I guess to get onto it, we'll have to drive around the block and get into the line-up at the top."

"Couldn't we just look at it?" Fred groaned. "Do we have to actually drive it? I don't know if our rather broad station wagon will be able to negotiate all those tight turns."

"Where's your sense of adventure, Fred? We've come all this way to see the sights. All those other wide American cars are managing. Of course we must give it a try."

Fred frowned with worry as Jacob's mom drove the station wagon along narrow one-way streets around the block and joined the line-up of other cars at the top of the "crookedest street in the world."

Jacob had moved to the back seat and was now sandwiched between the Finkle brothers. The Finkle sandwich position.

At least Barney wasn't practising his cow jokes at the moment.

"Come on," Jacob said. "Let's get this over with so we can get out of this roast-mobile and go to a park or something."

"Jacob," his mother said. "You're as impatient as a hot toad." She turned the station wagon and angled it down the street.

Minerva squealed and scrunched down in her seat. Would they make it?

The first section was narrow and the turns were sharp, but Jacob's mother expertly negotiated the broad car. They were about halfway down, creeping slowly now, with a long line of cars jammed up behind their bumper. As they approached a very sharp turn between two large planters overflowing with a mad tumble of flowers, Jacob drew in a deep breath. The big old station wagon slid between the wooden planters. Then plop, like a cork sucked into a bottle, it stuck there!

"Come on, Big Blue!" his mother urged. "You can make it." But she had the steering wheel pulled over as far as possible and she still couldn't get the broad car through. "Oh, dear! I should have turned sooner. We'll have to back up and try again."

Fred peered out the rearview mirror. "Festeration!" he exclaimed. "Look at that bloomin' line-up. Blimey! Bonnet to boot, all the way up the bloomin' hill!"

In spite of being worried, Jacob snorted and grinned at how Fred's English accent thickened when he got excited. He thought about Captain Haddock's "Billions of Blue Blistering Barnacles!"

"Here, Fred," Jacob's mother said. "You take the wheel and I'll go and tell those drivers they'll just have to back up." She pushed her door open and with a swish of her skirt, went to speak to the drivers of the cars behind. Minerva followed her.

Even with the windows open, the back seat of the car was hot and stuffy. Sam stunk. Jacob was sure he hadn't changed his clothes or brushed his teeth for days. Surely that was the same scruffy shirt he'd worn since the beginning of the trip.

Both Finkle brothers squirmed in their seats. They turned around, trying to get a better view of the action, and they poked Jacob with their sharp elbows and knees. Suddenly he couldn't stand being cooped up with them in that stuffy car for one more second.

"I'm getting out, too," he muttered. Reaching over Barney, he unlocked the door. He nudged Barney's shoulder. "Hey, man, I said I'm getting out!"

Barney grunted and shoved the door open.

Jacob scrambled out over him. He took a deep breath, expecting to smell the fresh colourful flowers that bordered the street, but got a nose full of smelly car fumes instead.

Barney followed Jacob outside and around the back of the car.

The bumper of the car behind them was less than a hand space from theirs. No wonder Big Blue couldn't make the turn, crowded like that.

Jacob's mother was waving her arms at the driver of the car behind. The driver was shaking his head. His friend beside him pointed to the car behind them, a shiny red convertible, and behind that was another car, and then another, as far as they could see, jamming up the crookedest street in the world. For all of them to back up would be impossible. Maybe they'd be stuck here all day. And all night.

One driver honked his horn and yelled, "What's the hold up? Come on. Get moving! We haven't got all day!"

Jacob's mother looked exasperated but determined. She smoothed down her skirt, walked up to the next car and started talking to the driver, her arms gesticulating wildly. Minerva followed her, now an embarrassed shadow.

Jacob leaned against the waist-high flower box beside the car. The box seemed to shift slightly under his weight. He looked at the next box and the next. They were about a meter high, made of wood, and maybe not permanently attached to the road. He shoved experimentally against the box with all his weight. It did move!

Could they shove aside the boxes enough to let the station wagon through the tight turn?

Fred was heading up the hill to help convince all the drivers they had to back up.

"If we moved these boxes a bit," Jacob called to him. "Maybe we could get the car past them."

Fred turned back. "What a bloomin' good idea! Here. Let's see how far we can push them." He joined Jacob and began shoving at the box. After heaving and straining, they managed to move it a foot or so.

Meanwhile, Barney was leaning against the car, watching them strain.

"Don't just stand there," Fred called out to him. "Come and give us a hand."

Barney reluctantly joined them. After a lot more heaving and struggling, they moved the six or so flower boxes that blocked the turn.

"Now let's give Big Blue a try," Fred said. He climbed back into the station wagon and started up the motor. It belched clouds of bluish smoke. Jacob turned away and coughed.

Big Blue slowly, ever so slowly, moved forward. The front bumper inched closer and closer to the flower boxes. It nicked against one on one side. Then one on the other.

"Still not enough room," Jacob reported.

Fred turned off the motor and came out to inspect. "So very close! Think we could move this one box just a bit more?"

"We can try," Jacob said.

Again they heaved with all their strength. But this box

seemed riveted to the ground. They were able to shift it only a few centimeters.

"Bloody hell! If there isn't enough bloomin' room now, I don't know what we'll do," Fred said, climbing back into the car.

Again he started the motor with a great cloud of fumes. The car edged forward slowly, slowly, the bumper just touching the flower box, nudging it, like Jacob sometimes nudged his soccer ball when he dribbled it down the field.

"Keep coming," Barney directed his dad. "Keep it coming."

There Barney was, directing traffic when it hadn't even been his idea or his work. Typical of him to take all the credit, Jacob noted.

The car slowly edged around the corner, the front bumper gently scraping, sliding by, one flower box, then the next, and the next. Around the corner slid the front bumper. It was like a slow-motion film. The bumper finally slipped past the last flower box.

"We made it!" Jacob shouted. "We're clear!"

"Great!" Fred said. "But let's push those boxes back to where they were."

He got out and helped Jacob heave the boxes back into place. Somehow it wasn't as difficult. It was as if the boxes knew their rightful places and were happy to be back.

"That was some excellent deductive reasoning there, Jacob," Fred said, flashing a wide smile in his direction. "A bloomin' good piece of creative problem solving. Sometimes the simplest solution is the one that works best.

Now, from an engineering standpoint, we often overlook the simplest and most obvious solutions."

Jacob thought that maybe Fred was going to stand there all day expounding. He nodded and said, "Sure, sure," and headed for the car. He grinned and thought maybe his mother was right. Maybe Fred was a nice guy. Awfully long-winded, but nice enough. Maybe.

As they all piled back into the car, Barney elbowed Jacob in the chest.

"Watch it, kid," Jacob grunted.

Barney stared at him blankly as if he hadn't done anything. But Jacob suspected Barney had elbowed him on purpose. And it seemed to him that Sam was even grumpier than usual. Could they be jealous that their father had praised him?

Jacob shrugged and fished his ball out of the back.

Minerva turned up her lively reggae music and Jacob bounced his ball on his knee in time with the steady beat. Frowning and muttering under his breath, Fred slowly, carefully negotiated the car to the bottom of the street, leaving a few streaks of fluorescent blue car paint behind on the flower boxes.

When they finally got to the bottom, he leaned on the horn and they all cheered. The couple in the car behind them honked and cheered too.

"I agree that must be the crookedest street possible!" Jacob's mom said, wiping her glistening brow with the sleeve of her blouse. "I wouldn't like to try that again.

You were right, Fred. We should have just looked at it."

Fred smiled at her. "But we made it. Thanks to that clever son of yours. Now how about lunch on the town to celebrate?"

Suddenly everyone was starving. They decided to head for nearby Chinatown.

The Chinatown streets were steep and narrow, but at least they were all straight. They were also clogged with cars and people. It seemed that everyone else in San Francisco wanted a Chinese lunch too. Fred shunted the car up and down the hot streets, while everyone watched for a parking space. They didn't find one that could accommodate a Mini, much less a lumpy old station wagon.

The hot rays of the noon-day sun reflected off the concrete sidewalks into the stuffy car. Jacob struggled to get a good breath. His chest felt clamped and nausea rolled over him.

"How about a picnic in Golden Gate Park instead?" his mother suggested.

"A bloomin' good idea," Fred said. He skillfully negotiated Big Blue through the crowded, narrow downtown streets, past high office buildings, past buses and clanging streetcars that stopped strangely, right in the middle of the busy streets, to disgorge passengers who then had to thread their precarious way through the erratic noon-hour traffic.

7

Eventually Big Blue shuddered to a stop beside a broad green field surrounded by tall leafy trees.

"Welcome to Golden Gate Park," Fred announced. "Gateway to our Picnic Paradise. It's our cool oasis in this choking city."

Jacob was about to push his way out of the car but he noticed some stitches in one of the seams on his ball had come loose. He bounced it against his knee. Was it a little less firm, less solid? Maybe it was suffocating in this heat like he was.

"Come on, man. Let's go," he said at last, nudging Sam with his elbow. He was bursting to get out into that wide grassy playing field and dribble his ball from one green end to the other.

But Sam just sat there blocking the door. He moved like a slug, slowly gathering up his action figures, winding his narrow fingers around each one. Barney got out his side, so Jacob scrambled after him instead.

He took a deep breath of the park air and let its freshness soak in. He was about to dribble his ball down the field when his mother said, "Come on, you big strong fellas. Before you take off, give me a hand with these picnic supplies."

Jacob rested his ball beside the car wheel and his mother loaded him and Barney up with blankets, water bottles, bags of buns, a large jar of peanut butter, a bag of grapes, and another of cookies. It was all the makings of their picnic.

"Reminds me of a riddle," Barney said.

"About cows?" Jacob asked.

"How'd you guess? Why do cows lie on their backs in a field?"

"Why?"

"To trip low flying birds."

"I knew that."

"Okay, here's another one: Do you know how long cows should be milked?"

"How long?"

"Same as short cows."

"Right, right," Jacob said. "How about setting the stuff in the shade under this tree?"

"Looks good to me."

They spread out the blankets and Jacob's mother sat at the edge of one, kicked off her sandals and wriggled her toes. "Now this is the life for me," she sighed.

Minerva turned on her boombox and fiddled with the dial, trying to find some decent music. "You'd think a big city li' San Francisco would have at least one good music station," she muttered. "But all they have are talk-talk shows and oldy-mouldy music." She popped in one of her own CDs, *Burning Spear*, and cranked up the volume for some good Jamaican reggae tunes.

Jacob jogged back to the car for his ball. He saw Sam sitting on it on the curb, whispering intently to his action figures.

"Okay, man. Get off my ball," Jacob told him. He nudged the ball with his foot none too gently.

When Sam unfolded himself from the ball, it wobbled slowly, drunkenly off the curb. There was a deep dent where Sam had been sitting on it!

Jacob gasped and scooped it up. Sure enough, his ball was completely caved in!

"You jerk!" he shouted at the kid. "Look what you've done!" He felt like he was about to explode. His ball, his ball! The one thing he had left from his dad. It was shrivelling up like a popped balloon!

"Didn't do nothing," Sam mumbled, sticking out his lower lip.

"But look at my ball! It's busted!" Jacob was yelling now. What right did the kid have touching his stuff?

Sam shrugged. "Didn't do nothing," he repeated. He turned and shuffled away, his hands full of sharp little toys.

"Come, boys," Jacob's mother called. "Lunch is ready."

Jacob wanted to kick the kid and punch his face with its stupid blank look. Blinking hard, he stumbled towards the picnic, cradling his lopsided ball.

His mother looked up from sorting the food. "Aren't you hungry, child?" Then she noticed the ball. "Oh, Jacob! What happened?"

"Sam sat on it," he said, his voice cracking.

"Come, sweet. Just sitting on a soccer ball wouldn't wreck it. You know that."

Jacob nodded reluctantly. "He probably poked a hole in the bladder with one of his action figure things."

"Did you?" Jacob's mom asked Sam as he wandered to the picnic blanket.

"Did I what?"

"Did you poke a hole in Jacob's ball?"

Sam shrugged and shook his head. "It was soft when I sat on it. That's all I did. Just sat on it."

Jacob glared at Sam through narrowed eyes. If Fred and his mother weren't there, he'd grab the kid and pound him.

Fred said, "Maybe we can pump it up again. I'll get the foot pump from the car."

Minerva cranked up the volume of her music while Jacob tried to pump up his ball. He knew it was a waste of time. He just knew it. He stamped angrily on the foot pump: down, up, down, up, down, up.

Why did his mother have to marry someone with such a dumb kid? Kids? Both were dunces. Freaky Finkles. Neither could kick a soccer ball worth a hill of beans. "Hunh?" was their favourite word.

Besides, they looked weird. Always stumbling over big long feet, wearing the same old cheesy clothes every day. If she had to marry someone, why couldn't it at least have been another Jamaican like his dad?

He got the ball hard, so hard the rubber bladder bulged

where the stitching was slack. But the air hissed out and soon it was as soft as ever.

Fred suggested that if they could somehow take the rubber bladder out of its leather case, they could probably patch it with a bicycle tube repair kit. But how would they get it stitched up again?

"Maybe we could tape it up with duct tape. It has excellent adhesive qualities, that duct tape," Fred said.

Jacob snorted. That sort of offer didn't deserve a reply. Fred obviously didn't know the first thing about soccer.

"We'll look for another ball for you, Jacob. Don't you worry now," his mother said. "There are lots of other soccer balls around."

"But this one's from Dad," he told her. He saw her frown slightly at the mention of his father. He knew she didn't like him talking about his dad around Fred. But he went on anyway. "Dad gave it to me for my birthday just before, you know, the car accident ..." A sob caught in his throat, but he swallowed hard and went on. "It's a genuine Supari. Some people know a lot about soccer. And some people just don't." He stared straight at Fred.

"Maybe we'll find a shopping centre this afternoon where you can buy another one," his mom went on.

"Don't you understand, Mom? I don't want another ball. I want this one. The one from my dad." His voice felt choked.

"Oh, Jay ..." His mother reached over to pat his shoulder, but he ducked away.

He couldn't eat much lunch. He sat under the tree with

his back to Sam and Fred, his shoulders hunched over his ball, cradling it on his lap like a sick child.

Minerva cranked up the reggae music even louder until Jacob could barely hear Fred shouting, "Rosa. Do we really need to have that music so bloomin' loud!"

"True. It's a bit loud, Minerva. Turn the volume down, my sweet."

Minerva snapped the CD out of the boombox and put it into her portable. Then she jammed on her earphones and cranked up the volume until the music swirled around her and formed a barrier between her and everyone else.

After lunch, Fred drained his lemonade and stretched out his long pale hairy legs. Although his nose was sunburned, his legs were still as white as raw bread dough. "That lunch certainly hit the spot," he said. "While we're here in the city, I'd like to go to the science centre. I've heard they have excellent hands-on exhibits and demonstrations at the Exploratorium. And they're all free with the price of admission."

Jacob looked at Minerva and wiggled his eyebrows. You'd never catch Fred passing up a bargain like that. Frugal Fred Finkle.

"I don't think I'll go," Jacob's mother said, folding up the blankets. "It's so beautiful out here in the park, I just want to walk around for a while and soak up this wonderful sunshine."

"I don't feel like going around any museum either,"

Minerva said. "What about you, Jay?"

"Yeah, I'll walk around the park too," he mumbled.

"Right-o. We'll meet back here at the car in a couple of hours? Say around four?" Fred said, getting up to leave with his boys.

"Fine, but no later," Jacob's mother said. "It'll take us long enough to get out of the city in rush hour."

After putting the picnic supplies back into the car, Jacob followed his mother and Minerva. They strolled through the park towards the Japanese Tea Gardens. Tall trees of every sort were on either side of the path. Soon they found a protected spot of shade.

"Can I have a dollar for ice cream?" Minerva asked.

"Hmm," their mother said, settling down in the shade and opening her purse. "The question of money. I've been thinking about it. How about I give you each forty dollars?"

"Forty bucks? Sure!" Minerva said. "What's the catch?"

"That will be ten dollars a week and it has to last you the rest of the trip. You have to promise not to ask me for any more money until we get home. Not one penny. It's time you both learned to become more financially responsible. So, is that agreed?"

"Sure thing," Minerva said, putting her two twenties into her wallet.

Jacob nodded and took his. "Agreed."

"Don't look so sad, Jay," his mom said, patting his hand.

Jacob shook his head. "Those two Finkle kids just bug me so much," he said. "They're such nerds."

"Be kind, Jacob," his mother said. "They're both very nice little boys."

"Humph!" he snorted. "Nice! I've never seen such weird kids. All Sam ever does is sit around moping and playing with those stupid little action figure things."

"I think Barney and Sam might be missing their mother. Especially Sam. He was awfully young when his mom and dad divorced and he doesn't get to see her very often. By the way, I think I better warn you two. Fred and I have been discussing whether to go to Los Angeles. He thinks Disneyland and Universal Studios are a lot of commercial hype. A waste of good money. Besides, because of this heat spell, there's a bad smog alert there now. So we've decided to bypass L.A. and head straight to San Diego from here."

"What! Bypass L.A!" Minerva cried. "L.A.'s the only reason I came on this stupid trip. Every one of my friends has been to L.A. and they all say it's the greatest. You wanted to go there too, Mom. You said so. Can't you change Fred's mind? You've got to!"

"I don't think so. Maybe he's right. I mean, it's so hot here in San Francisco, imagine how unpleasant it must be in an even bigger city like L.A. with the smog alert and everything." She raked her fingers through the hair at the back of her neck and opened her book.

Minerva shook her head. "I can't believe it, Mom. Letting Fred boss you around like that. I would never let anyone boss me around. Ever."

"But I agree with him, girl. Truly, I do. We can't do everything this time. We'll save L.A. for another trip."

"I knew I shouldn't have come on this lousy trip." Minerva scowled and jammed on her earphones again. "I'm going for a walk."

She stomped away down the tree-lined path that led into some woods. Her arms were crossed tightly, angrily. Jacob started to follow her.

"Be sure to be back at the car before four," his mom called after them. "And don't get lost. You two stick together now."

He gave her a thumbs up sign and dropped his lopsided ball to the ground. He nudged it gently, rolling it, trying to keep it from wobbling off the path, which took them into a woods of tall trees, leafy shrubs and ferns.

8

After a while Jacob heard music drifting through the woods. Twanging guitar, a throbbing bass, a solid drum beat. It was a familiar beat. The syncopated, complex beat of reggae music. Minerva had her earphones on and her CD player turned up high so she mustn't be able to hear the music. He nudged his ball onto her feet.

She frowned at him over her shoulder.

"Music," he told her. "Reggae music."

She took off her earphones.

"What?"

"Can't you hear the music?"

Drifting through the trembling leaves of the tall trees overhead came the beat of drums and the lilt of someone singing.

Her scowl broke into a broad grin.

"Hey, man! What are we waiting for?" she whooped. "Let's go!"

Lured by the magnetic music, they raced along the path. When they emerged from the woods, they saw a shallow, bowl-shaped field below with an outdoor theatre at its edge. Members of a reggae band, dressed in colourful clothes, were swaying on the stage.

"All right!" Minerva breathed, her dark eyes glistening. She grinned at Jacob. It was like her best dream coming true. A real live reggae band right there in the middle of the park.

They sprinted down the grassy knoll and threaded through an audience lounging on blankets. Minerva joined a bunch of teenagers dancing in front of the stage while Jacob stood at the edge and watched. Music throbbed in the warm air, sending waves of sound over them. An ocean of sound drenched them. Minerva fell into the music like she was plunging into a refreshing pool of water. She spun, her eyes shut, whirling, twirling, leaping, her pale purple skirt and long black hair swaying in time with the hypnotic sounds.

The band played one tune, then another, faster and louder. The lead singer's voice pleaded with them to "stand up for your rights."

The excitement of the music grew until it blared. The hypnotic beat seeped into Jacob's head, into his body. He swayed back and forth, pulsating in time. The beat became his beat, his breath beat, his own heartbeat.

Minerva swirled and swayed. She leapt between the other dancers like a butterfly, a dragonfly. Higher and higher she leapt, her skirt swirling about her like wings. It seemed as if the earth's gravity had lost its effect on her.

The music mounted to a climax. Then it stopped.

"That's all for today, folks," the singer shouted to the clapping, cheering crowd. The dancers sighed. They gathered up their things and started drifting away.

The singer was tall and young and good-looking. He swung back his long dreadlocks, his heavy, ringlet-like hair. His white shirt was open in front revealing a heaving brown chest, glistening with sweat.

Minerva remained in front of the stage gazing raptly at him, her hands clasped. The singer bent forward to talk to her. She smiled up at him and nodded. Then she followed him backstage.

Where was she going? Jacob wondered. He moved quickly, not letting her out of his sight. Behind the stage, the band members and their friends had congregated in an open tent. They were drinking and pouring ice water over each other. The water flowed down their faces and necks, soaking their shirts, plastering the cloth to their backs. Laughing, they wagged their heads like playful dogs, showering each other.

Jacob spotted his sister talking to the singer.

"Come on, Min," he said. "We got to head back."

"In a minute, Jay."

"Who's this?" the tall singer asked, smiling a wide friendly smile.

"My brother, Jacob," Minerva told him.

"Aha. Soccer player, I see," the singer said, indicating Jacob's ball. "Maybe we could kick it around a bit?"

Jacob held up his ball. "It's flat," he said.

"Ah brotha'. Compared wit' what we play wit' back home in Jamaica, that ball's terrific. Hey, man, you ever hear of Pelé, the most famous soccer player this world has ever seen?"

"Course."

"He would have loved this ball when he was a kid. It's lots better than what I had when I was growing up in Jamaica. Back home we use any round thing at all. A grapefruit, an orange. Even a bunch of rags all stuffed into a sock. Compared to what we use in Jamaica, man, this ball is terrific! Here, give us a pass now."

Jacob dropped the ball to his foot and nudged it to the tall singer who deftly passed it back.

"Hey, what you got there?" asked one of the other musicians, a short, dark complexioned young man. Jacob recognized him as the drummer.

"One kick-ball game coming up," the singer announced.

The drummer nodded. "Ting bout playin' this music is energy," he told Jacob. "Energy! It leave you wit' so much energy. You got to do someting wit' all that energy." The way he said "energy" was like "energeeeee."

Jacob grinned at him. The drummer sounded like his dad used to, after he'd had a couple of beers. That's when he'd slip into his back-home, Jamaican accent. His mother, on the other hand, used her Jamaican voice only when she was angry.

The drummer kicked Jacob's ball. It wobbled back and forth to the other band members. Jacob got into the scrimmage and soon had his ball back, but someone nudged it away from him again. It wobbled crazily from foot to foot, this way and that, everyone trying to get the ball away.

They quickly formed two teams: Minerva, the lead singer, whose name was Amos, and the drummer on one team, and Jacob and the rest of the band members on the other. Jacob wasn't sure what instrument, they played. Guitars, maybe? Or was that guy with the long blond hair the bass player?

Back and forth, up and down the field they dribbled the wobbly ball, scoring goal after goal. No one kept score, but when it was about ten to ten, the drummer yelled, "Time! Hey, man. I got to take a rest."

They all plunked down on the cool grass in the shade at the edge of the field.

"So where is the lovely young lady heading?" Amos asked, panting, sprawled at Minerva's feet.

"Mexico," she told him. She was panting too and her forehead glistened with sweat. She blew a wisp of hair away.

"No kidding! That's what you can do with that ball then," he said to Jacob who sat cradling his ball between his knees.

"What?"

"Those kids in Mexico. You think we had it rough in Jamaica? Or Pelé had it rough in Brazil? Man! They got it so bad down there in Mexico, some kids never see a real football once in their whole entire life! You know what they'd do with this ball of yours? They'd take out the bladder inside and fix it up with some patches and some glue, like.

Then they'd ask their grandmama to sew it up all nice. They'd make the whole ball like new again."

The drummer nodded. "True. Just like new."

Jacob nodded too. He stroked his ball and thought, yes! That's what he'd do when they got to Mexico. Then he glanced at his watch. "Oh no! Look at the time, Min! They'll all be at the car waiting for us. We should have left ages ago."

"You have to go?" Amos asked Minerva, frowning. "Why don't you stay with us? We're looking for some good-looking sisters for dancers. Come. Travel with us for a while. We've got a gig up in Canada in a couple of weeks. We could drop you home then, if you want."

Minerva gazed at him and nodded. "Sounds fantastic. So fantastic. Let's, Jay. Travelling with these guys would sure beat being cooped up in that stuffy old station wagon."

"You know Mom would never let us," Jacob said.

People around them were packing up, loading equipment and instruments into a dusty van, preparing to leave. Amos strummed his guitar, humming softly, gazing at Minerva, serenading her. She gazed back at him. Soon she was swaying in time to his music, as if she'd forgotten all about leaving.

"Min. Come on. We've got to go," Jacob pleaded. He plucked at her sleeve.

She ignored him. She had that same entranced, far-away stare she got sometimes when she was plugged into her stereo earphones. She wouldn't even look his way now. It was as if Amos was hypnotizing her. What could Jacob do?

"Well, I'm heading back," he told her loudly, and slowly walked away. She'll follow once I start leaving, he thought.

But she didn't. When he turned back, Minerva was still there in front of Amos, gazing stupidly up at him.

"Minerva!" Jacob yelled.

She didn't even glance at him.

"Mom. I've got to get Mom!" he mumbled to himself. He dashed across the field, up the knoll, through the woods, along the path and back to the car.

"There you are!" Fred said. "Do you know what time it is? We'd almost given up on you two."

"Mom! Where's Mom?"

"She's gone to look for you. A tad worried, she was, now it's so late. Where's your sister?"

"She, she won't come back!" Jacob cried, looking wildly about for his mother. What if Amos and his band all left? And took Minerva with them! Kidnapped her! Maybe that's what they did. Went about the countryside, luring young girls with their music, then kidnapping them … "We've got to get her back now!"

"I'll come and talk to her," Fred said. "Doesn't she realize she's holding us up? You boys stay right here," he said to his sons. "If Rosalina comes back, tell her we've found Minerva. Now where's that sister of yours?"

Jacob led Fred through the woods. What good would Fred be? Minerva was already furious at him for not letting them go to L.A.

When Minerva saw them approaching, she ducked behind the van. Jacob knew she was trying to disappear into the crowd of musicians.

But Fred followed her behind the van, his head stuck forward, his large nose red. "Come now, Minny," he said, his voice loud and stern. "Did you see the time? We're all waiting at the car. Your mother's becoming very worried."

No, no. Don't call her Minny, thought Jacob. She hates that name so much!

Minerva stared at Fred. Wild bristly beard, shiny red nose, knobby knees. She flushed with embarrassment.

"Come now, Minny," he repeated, reaching for her arm.

She yanked away. "I don't have to do what you say," she hissed at him. "You're not the boss of me! You, you …"

"Minerva!"

Jacob and Minerva wheeled around to see their mother descend upon them, with whirling skirts and dark flashing eyes.

The whole crew, including Amos, sort of melted away before her wrath. They recognized a woman on the warpath. Even Jacob ducked behind some barrels.

"Minerva! There you are! You're late! We've been waiting on you. Fred. What are you doing here?"

Before Fred could answer, Minerva wailed, "Mom, it's all so boring, this whole car trip's so boring. And now that we're not even going to L.A. there's no reason for me to be on it. Amos here says his band has a gig in Vancouver in a couple of weeks. I've decided to go back home with them."

"What!" exploded her mother. "My daughter travel around the countryside wit' God knows who? Come, girl. What you thinkin' about? You think I'd let my own child travel around wit' a bunch of scalawags like these? It's bad enough we had to wait for you and your brotha'." Her voice rose and her accent thickened. She looked as if she was about to grab her daughter, by the ear if necessary, and drag her away. Her cheeks grew red and her frizzy hair stood on end as if she'd been struck by a jolt of lightning.

"But, but ..." Minerva tried to interrupt but her mother went on.

"You comin' wit' us, girl, right now, if I have to carry you off meself wit' these two hands."

Minerva looked as if she wished she could drop dead right there and then from embarrassment. Her new friends avoided looking at her and drifted away.

"Ah, Rosalina," Fred interrupted, putting his arm around her shoulder. "Rosa, my dear. Perhaps we could all talk this over quietly on our way back to the car? We'll be back in Vancouver in a few weeks so perhaps Minerva's new friends could get in touch with her then? Right, Minerva?"

Minerva looked at Fred gratefully. She nodded. There was a way out. This horrible embarrassment could end.

"Okay," she mumbled, kicking at the ground. "Let's go back to the car."

Jacob glanced back at the vans. Amos was nowhere in sight. He too had evaporated.

9

On the way back to their campsite, Minerva sat in the back seat of the car, crunched into her corner. Even from the front seat where he was sitting, Jacob could almost smell her smouldering. He agreed with her about missing L.A. and Disneyland. With her earphones jammed on, Minerva stared glassy-eyed out the window. Even when they stopped at a fruit stand, she just stayed in her seat.

Fred bought a fat green watermelon for supper and they continued along the highway.

"We'll find a sports store for you tomorrow on our way south," Jacob's mother promised him. "They'll have so many balls to choose from, you won't be able to make up your mind."

"Humph," Jacob said, stroking the dented ball on his lap. Chances of replacing it were pretty darn slim. Besides, even if they did find a new ball, he was going to hang onto this one forever.

It was the boys' turn to make supper so they decided to do something simple: hamburgers and beans. After trying for a couple of minutes to get Sam to help with the easy parts of the food preparation, Barney gave up and told him that he would have to do all the washing-up instead.

Sam shrugged, pointed the gun of one of his action figures at Barney and said, "Bang, bang."

Barney turned his back on Sam and started frying the meat patties in the big cast iron frying pan on the camp stove, while Jacob chopped up the lettuce, and sliced the tomatoes and pickles. Then he stirred up a bowl of a special sauce made out of mayonnaise, relish and catsup. They put it all on the picnic table with a large container of apple juice.

"Sure does look good," Barney said. "Reminds me of a joke. Where do little cows eat their lunch at school?"

"Where?" Jacob said.

"In the Calf-eteria. Get it? Calf? Calf-eteria?"

"Right," Jacob said, nodding and trying not to yawn in Barney's face.

"What a wonderful meal!" Jacob's mother said. "You boys will certainly win the meal of the year award."

"Excellent, without a doubt. Bravo, boys," Fred agreed, wiping sauce from his beard with his handkerchief. He was well into his second helping.

Supper had turned out amazingly well, thought Jacob. Maybe Barney could do something besides tell bad cow jokes. He was thinking about going for his third burger when he remembered the watermelon.

He got it from the car and sawed it open with the bread knife. The firm pink flesh smelled so delicious that his mouth watered in spite of his stomach feeling full with burgers. He sawed the whole thing into thick juicy slices and settled in to demolish his share.

After the last piece of melon was devoured, Fred reminded them to wash up their own dishes. "And since you didn't help produce this magnificent feast, Sam, you have the honour of washing out the frying pan and doing garbage duty. That means find all the garbage, put it into this garbage bag, then throw it out into the dumpster. Agreed?"

Sam nodded, absently gnawing a melon rind.

Fred and Jacob's mother left, arm in arm for their usual evening stroll to watch the sun set.

"Again!" Jacob thought. "They just saw it last night." He sat on the picnic bench and stroked his dented ball. It was flatter than ever.

"Want to go check out the video games in the games room?" Barney asked him.

"No," Jacob shook his head. "I don't think so."

"Want to go for a swim, then?"

"No cow jokes?"

"What do you mean, no cow jokes?"

"No cow jokes," Jacob repeated.

"Okay, okay. No cow jokes."

"All right! No cow jokes! You coming for a swim, Min?"

"Okay, I guess," she sighed. "Anything's got to be better than just sitting around here." Although everyone else had eaten a huge supper, she had just picked at her food.

"No point asking Squirt to come along," Barney said. "It'll take him at least another hour to wash his plate and the hamburger pan and throw out the garbage. Hey, Squirt. Don't forget to pick up all the garbage, including all the watermelon rinds and everything."

Sam continued chewing his watermelon rind and didn't say anything.

Jacob left his ball on the picnic-table seat beside the big plastic garbage bag. He and Barney and Minerva grabbed towels and bathing suits and strolled over to the pool.

There were only a couple of other people in the pool, adults doing lengths. Jacob slid in at the deep end. After the first shock of the cool water against his skin, he turned onto his back and floated, gazing up at the purple sky, the water gurgling in his ears.

Barney jumped in, just missing Jacob's face by centimeters and splashing water up his nose.

"Hey!" Jacob grabbed a flipper from the side of the pool and splashed so much water right into Barney's face, he had to beg for mercy.

After they fooled around in the water for a while and did a couple of laps, the pool became crowded with a bunch of screeching little kids. Jacob pulled himself out of the water. "I'm going to have a shower, then head back to camp," he said.

"Okay," Minerva agreed. "I'll come too."

Barney followed them out of the pool. After good long

hot showers they dried off and changed, and ambled back to their camp. It was getting dark now and their way was lit by the glowing lamps on picnic tables. The air was still warm and smelled of campfires and freshly chopped wood.

When they got back to their campsite, Sam was still there alone, absently scrubbing the frying pan in a bowl of soapy water. He was really playing with the bubbles more than scrubbing.

Jacob went automatically to the picnic table for his ball. But the ball wasn't there! He searched in the deep shadows under the bench, under the table. His ball wasn't there either! He swallowed hard and started breathing fast. It *had* to be around here somewhere. He grabbed the car door handle and yanked the door open.

"So much junk in here," he muttered, rummaging around the back seat in the dim light. He couldn't see his ball. "Where is it? Where is it?" He slammed the door shut, raced to his tent and dove in. He thrashed through his stuff and Minerva's, squinting his eyes in the dim light. No ball there either.

He was feeling really frantic now. He dashed to the picnic table and shouted, "You guys seen my ball?"

Minerva was sitting on the table, plugged into her earphones, as usual. She shook her head.

Barney shook his head too and went on poking at the dead campfire.

"Hey, Squirt, you seen my soccer ball?" he asked Sam. His voice came out sounding tight, strained.

"Soccer ball?" Sam said, blinking up at him. "You mean that beat-up old ball that was on the bench by the picnic table? You mean that one?"

"That's the one," Jacob muttered, his stiff lips barely moving.

"Well, um," Sam said, squeezing dirty dish water out of a sponge. He was still scrubbing the same pan. "Dad told me to pick up all the garbage and put it in the garbage bag. I didn't think you wanted that old busted-up ball any more so I put it in the garbage bag." He shrugged.

"You what!" Jacob clenched his fist. "So where's that garbage bag now?" He scanned the picnic site but couldn't see a plastic garbage bag anywhere.

"I threw it away already. Dad said I had to throw out the garbage and ..."

"But it was *my* ball! You threw away *my* ball! That's not garbage!" He leapt at Sam.

Sam cringed away and Barney jumped between them to protect his little brother.

Fred and Jacob's mother appeared out of the gloom.

"What's happening here?" Fred said.

"Sam! He — he threw my ball away in the garbage!" Jacob's throat was tight. He was almost sobbing.

"Is that true?" Fred asked Sam. "You threw away Jacob's soccer ball?"

Sam blinked up at his dad, then nodded.

"We'll get it, Jacob. Sam. Leave that silly pan at once and show us exactly where you put that garbage bag."

Sam wiped his soapy hands on the front of his shirt. His father marched him towards the garbage drop-off. Jacob followed them to a large metal dumpster. It was almost as high as the top of his head. Barney trailed close behind.

"I tossed the bag in here," Sam said. "It was hard, but I got it in after a couple of tries."

The smell was nauseating.

"Which side?" Fred asked.

"I think it was over here. Maybe this side."

Jacob held onto the metal edge of the dumpster and pulled himself up. Barney jumped up beside him. They peered over the edge. Although the smell was almost overpowering, the container was nearly empty. In the glow of the overhead street light, Jacob could see some loose garbage strewn on the bottom: empty beer cans, used paper plates, rotting vegetables. But no plastic garbage bags. And no soccer ball.

"It — it's not here," Jacob told Fred. His voice wouldn't stop wobbling. "There aren't any garbage bags in there at all."

"What?" Fred peered over the edge and saw that what Jacob said was true. "I thought you said you put our bag of garbage in here, Sam."

"I did," Sam nodded. "But the garbage truck already hauled it away. I watched them do it."

"What! Why didn't you tell us?"

"I was going to, but you didn't let me."

"Blood and guts! I sometimes wonder if you ever think. You spend all day just dreaming. Didn't you know that was Jacob's ball?"

Sam nodded. "But he said it was busted. It wasn't any good anymore."

"You know you shouldn't touch things that don't belong to you," Fred admonished.

Sam didn't say anything. He just stared at the ground.

"Come on," Fred said. "Let's go back to the campsite." He shook his head and turned to Jacob. "Sorry about that, Jacob. We'll try and get you a new ball tomorrow."

"But, but …" Jacob's voice choked up. He couldn't go on. He felt like sobbing. Nobody understood that it wasn't just any old ball. It was the ball his father had given him. The last thing he'd given him before that terrible accident.

10

That night Jacob was rolled up in his sleeping bag thinking about his ball. He wished he could have told the little jerk to keep his paws off his stuff. That if he so much as looked at his stuff again, he would pound him into a pulp. But he couldn't say anything with Fred standing right there.

The other reason Jacob couldn't say anything was because of a very large lump in his throat. He was glad it had been dark out or everyone would probably have thought the water overflowing his eyes was tears. He just didn't know what he'd do without his ball.

As he was tossing about in his sleeping bag, Minerva whispered, "Jay? Jay? You asleep?"

"Um?" he muttered.

"Do you think he'll write me? Do you think he'll call when they get to Vancouver?"

"Who?"

"You know. Amos. That singer."

"Probably not."

"Oh you! He's so-oo handsome, don't you think? And

what a great singer! I just love his music," Minerva sighed. "Hope he doesn't lose my address and phone number. I can't wait until we get back home."

Late in the night someone tripped over the tent guy-line and woke Jacob. He put his face close to the fine screen window and peered out into the darkness. He couldn't see anyone. Since he was awake, he decided to visit the wash-room. He pulled on his jeans and shoes.

The full moon coloured the grass and bushes a strange, pale greyish-green. The moon was so bright, it cast his shadow on the sandy road in front of him.

Someone else was walking along the road a few campsites ahead. After a moment, he recognized Sam's stiff-legged shuffle. So maybe Sam had to go to the washroom too. It was probably he who had tripped over the tent guy-line.

Jacob walked behind him, not bothering to catch up. Sam kept glancing nervously, this way and that, but he didn't look back.

Jacob was surprised when Sam walked right past the men's toilets. Surely he wouldn't make a mistake and go into the women's? Could he be sleep walking? If he was, Jacob didn't feel like following him. He wasn't the brat's babysitter. Should he go back and wake Fred and tell him? But if he did, maybe by the time Fred found Sam, he would have fallen into the pool and drowned and it would be all Jacob's fault. Good riddance, he thought. On the other hand, maybe he should follow the kid to keep an eye on him, in case he did anything stupid.

Should he call out to Sam and wake him up? Somewhere in the back of Jacob's mind he had an idea that you should never wake a sleepwalker. You could seriously disturb them or something if you woke them too suddenly. But then, maybe that's exactly what sulky-Sam needed. A big jolt.

Sam continued walking down the road leading out of the KOA camp. Now he was heading toward the highway. Jacob quickened his pace. If the kid wandered onto the highway, one of those huge transport trucks could run him down. Flat, splat, all over the asphalt.

But no, he turned off on another road, a road even narrower and less travelled than the one leading to the highway. Jacob kept following him down the hill. He was gaining on him now. Where was the kid heading?

Then Jacob knew. The odour on the night breeze blowing past them was unmistakable. He was heading for the dump.

When Jacob caught up to him, Sam had his head thrust deep into a garbage bag, already searching through it. His head jerked up and he stared at Jacob, his round eyes glittering with fear.

So he wasn't sleepwalking after all, thought Jacob.

"Hey, Sam," he said. "What are you doing here? Don't you know it's the middle of the night?"

"Oh, it's just you, Jay." There was huge relief in the little boy's voice. "I'm trying to find your ball. It's got to be in one of these bags somewhere."

"What? You came out here in the middle of the night all by yourself? To find my ball?" Jacob shook his head. "Weren't you scared?"

"I brought my Seraptor for protection. He's my most fierce action figure." Sam held out one of his toys, the vicious looking fighter with bulging muscles. "But I'm glad you're here now, Jacob. You're a big kid."

He looked up at Jacob with trust and admiration. Jacob felt about three inches taller. "You really think my ball's here?" he said, his heart quickening.

Sam nodded.

Jacob pounced on the garbage bags, pulled one open and started searching.

At first, he expected to find his ball in each bag he opened. He gingerly poked through the smelly contents: used paper plates, dripping tin cans, squashed fruit and rotting vegetables. When he saw the bag didn't contain his ball, he did it up neatly again before tossing it back onto the pile. His ball was bound to be here. It had to be here. They would come across it any minute. Good, good, good! He couldn't wait to hold it in his arms again. But as they worked their way through the pile, Jacob became more and more desperate. He ended up spilling the bags and kicking through the debris. The more bags he dumped out, the more his elation trickled away.

Finally, after searching what felt like at least a hundred bags, he shook his head. "It's just not here, Sam. Maybe they dumped our garbage somewhere else."

"Sorry about your ball, Jay. You could have my Seraptor if you want." Sam offered his favourite toy. "I've got lots of other ones."

"No, that's okay. You keep your Seraptor. Maybe we'd better head back to camp."

Jacob turned and stumbled over a garbage bag that had toppled off the pile. He kicked it in frustration. The wire tie burst off and out tumbled a bunch of watermelon rinds. And then … he could not believe it! His ball, his ball, his precious ball!

He grabbed it up and pressed it close to his chest. Even covered with garbage, even squashed and flat and smelly, it felt wonderful, the smooth leather against his chin. At last, he thought. He took in a deep breath and hugged it again, thinking of hugging his dad.

They headed back to their campsite, Sam striding by Jacob's side. Sam didn't look one bit scared now. In fact, he was staring up at Jacob with such confidence that Jacob found that he was striding along too. No, he was strutting, his shoulders shoved back, his back tall and straight, ready to protect this little kid from the unseen dangers of the night.

The next morning, Jacob woke late. Minerva was already up. He rubbed his eyes and yawned as he pushed his way out of the tent. Good, he thought. Another sunny day. He automatically started taking down the tent, pulling the pegs out of the ground.

Barney was helping his dad load up the storage box on top the car.

"But, Da-ad," Jacob heard him whine. "We've got to go to L.A. We just have to. That's where Disneyland and Universal Studios are. You promised!"

"Blood and guts, Barnaby! I did not promise. As far as I'm concerned, L.A. with all its bloomin' Disneyland and Hollywood hype is the epitome of American commercialism at its very worst. Certainly something we can live without, at the moment. Pass me that tent, now."

"But Disneyland is really very educational, Dad. You can learn all about space and dinosaurs and a whole lot of other things too."

"We can get books that will do the same thing. There's no point arguing. We simply are not going. And that's that. Not on this trip anyway."

"But what about Rosa? She said she wanted to go. She was going to show us all how to dance at the bandstand in Disneyland, remember?"

His dad smiled. "Since when were you interested in dancing?"

"I'm not, but —but …" Barney shook his head. Somehow he'd run out of arguments.

"There'll be enough dancing for us when we get to Mexico. You'll see. This way it'll give us more time there and we'll get there all the sooner. We'll have plenty of time for exploring a foreign culture. Sampling all that wonderful Mexican food, listening to the music, soaking in all the sights …"

Minerva's boombox was playing Jamaican music full blast and Jacob's mother was making tortillas for breakfast.

"I just don't know how much more 'foreign' culture I can take," Barney mumbled as he shuffled back to get his tent.

11

A few days later, Jacob and his family finally arrived at the Mexican border crossing. Before actually entering Mexico, they decided to do some last minute shopping at a border shopping centre.

The first thing Jacob looked for when they entered the department store was the sporting goods section. He still had not found a new soccer ball. Not that he wanted to replace his old one. He planned to keep that one forever. But his toe twitched and his head ached to bounce a good solid ball off his forehead. Kick, kick, kick. How he longed to be out in some field whipping it up.

Before Minerva and Jacob went to check out the sports department, their mother caught them by the shoulders. She lowered her head and whispered, "It's going to be Barney's birthday in a few days. How about looking for a gift for him?"

Jacob said, "Us?"

"Sure. It would be a good surprise, don't you think?"

"Okay," Minerva shrugged. She put her hands in her pockets and started down the aisle towards sporting goods.

"I'll get some groceries, then meet you at the car in about twenty minutes," their mother said.

Jacob nodded and sauntered after Minerva. "Thought you were mad at the Finkles," he said.

She shrugged again. "Just because I'm mad at Fred for making us miss L.A. doesn't mean we can't buy the kid a birthday present."

Soon it became clear that "Sporting Goods" in the store meant fishing and hunting equipment. Not one soccer ball in sight. Jacob couldn't see even a basketball.

A sales clerk wearing a blue jacket was rearranging some fishing gear. He had yellowish buck-teeth and a large red nose. He kept sniffing loudly.

"Excuse me," Jacob said. "Do you have any soccer balls?"

"Ah, soccer?" Sniff, sniff. "Ah, no soccer. Sorry, sonny."

Jacob could tell that the clerk probably wasn't sure what a soccer ball looked like.

"What about in that basket up there?" Jacob pointed to a large plastic basket of balls on a high shelf.

"Doubt if you'd find one in there, sonny. We get some in the fall sometimes, but not much demand for — uh — soccer balls this time of the year." The clerk sniffed a long gurgly sniff and turned away to continue rearranging the fishing rods.

The basket on the high shelf was full to the brim with every type and colour and pattern of ball imaginable. Large beach balls, baseballs, tiny bouncy balls. Jacob's toe felt so empty with nothing to nudge around. There just might be a soccer ball in that basket. At this point, he'd settle for even an imitation, baby-sized one, as long as it was something he could kick around.

"Maybe we could just take a look?" Jacob said to the clerk's back.

"You're gonna have to take my word for it, sonny," the clerk sniffed. "No soccer balls in that basket. Anyway, I got too much work to do, to waste time taking it down." Sniff, sniff.

Jacob turned away, disappointed. Would he ever find a ball? But here they were, almost in Mexico. Surely he'd find a good ball there.

He was about to wander back to the car when Minerva said, "The kid's present, remember?"

Jacob nodded. His eyes fell on an inexpensive badminton set: two racquets, a couple of birds and a net. He picked it up.

"What do you think?" he asked Minerva.

"Sure," she shrugged. "Good as anything."

Glancing down the aisle, they spotted Barney with his dad in deep conversation over the model airplane motors in the toy section. Minerva waved Jacob back.

"We want to buy this without Barney seeing it. It's meant to be a surprise," she whispered to him.

Jacob swung the badminton set behind his back.

"They're coming this way!" she hissed out of the side of her mouth. "Better stash it away somewhere."

Jacob shoved the set up onto a high shelf.

"Still shows," Minerva whispered.

So he shoved it farther into the shelf.

Suddenly there was a loud crash on the other side of the aisle, and the sound of hundreds of bouncing balls.

Oh no! He must have pushed something off the shelf on the other side when he was trying to hide the racquets. The basket full of balls!

He dashed to the next aisle. Sure enough, balls of every description were rolling and bouncing around! He fell to his knees, trying to catch one ball, then another. Minerva slid around trying to help.

The toothy, red-nosed clerk loomed over them. "What's going on here? What do you kids think you're doing with all those balls?" he demanded, spitting angrily.

Jacob stood up and buried his hands in his pockets. "Balls? What balls?" He tripped over a small bouncy ball. "Oh! You mean these balls? From the basket? You were right." He shrugged and smiled widely. "No soccer balls there."

As he backed out of the sporting goods department, he signalled to Minerva. She snuck down the aisle after him. They zipped past the cashiers and out the exit. Then they made a beeline for Big Blue. It was easy to spot in the crowded parking lot with the kayak and the colourful storage box on the roof.

Breathlessly, Jacob and Minerva ducked behind the car. Then they burst out laughing.

"Have you ever seen such a nerd? Dah ... what's a going on here, sonny? Sniff, sniff ... dah ... a ball?" Jacob mimicked the clerk.

Minerva giggled. "Soccer ball? What's a soccer ball? Sniff, sniff."

Their mother was not pleased when she returned with a large bag of groceries and heard they hadn't bought anything for Barney's birthday. She leaned the heavy bag on the car's hood and said, "You mean in that whole big store, you couldn't find one thing an eleven-year-old would like?"

"No cows," Minerva shrugged.

Jacob had to stifle his giggles. If their mother heard about the ball incident, she'd march them right back into the store to apologize and pick up every last ball. So he tried to straighten his face but he saw that Minerva was struggling too. That made him lose it. His giggles burst out in loud guffaws.

"Maybe we can find something more interesting for him when we get to Mexico," Minerva tried to say, but that made them laugh even more.

Fred and his boys returned so that ended the discussion. They all climbed into the hot car. It was Jacob's turn to sit in the least favourite position again, the middle of the back seat between the Finkle brothers. But at least they were almost in Mexico.

The Mexico–U.S. border crossing was a disappointment. Jacob was not sure what he had expected. Maybe lights, maracas, music, Spanish guitars. And at least some evidence of Mexico's national sport, soccer. The crossing was marked by a flimsy wooden building and a grinning uniformed man who waved them on by. He didn't even stop them to ask the usual questions: Where were you born? Where do you live? What's the purpose of your visit?

Jacob craned his neck to find a soccer field. Now that they were actually in Mexico, where were all the kids playing soccer? The landscape was almost the same as north of the border in the U.S.A., except maybe dustier and grimier. There were a few small houses and stores, some dusty trees, a few gas stations with GAZ on them. Must be Spanish for gas, thought Jacob. But not one park in sight. Maybe when they got closer to a town?

As they approached Tijuana, Jacob kept a sharp lookout. So where were the parks? The empty lots? The kids kicking around a grapefruit, an old sock full of rags? He saw nothing like that. There were rows of unpainted houses, old cars, dilapidated buildings, dirty roads and a large open air market. His mom and Fred debated whether to stop at the market and decided to drive away from the border, and down the coast to more interesting towns.

Good. Surely they would soon find some great soccer games there.

12

The Mexican highway was an ordinary two-lane road, quite different from the sleek divided American freeways. Every few kilometres they had to stop to pay a toll of a few pesos. At one stop, Jacob unfastened his seat belt and searched around behind the seat for his pack. He accidentally elbowed Barney in the stomach.

"Sorry," he muttered when Barney groaned.

He dug out his ball and a ballpoint pen. He smoothed out the leather of the ball and wrote on it in big block letters: Jelé Armstrong, Vancouver, Canada.

"Hey, that reminds me about another cow joke," Barney said.

Jacob groaned.

"If ten cows run after six cows, what time is it?"

"What?"

"Ten after six. Milking time."

Jacob nodded and went on writing.

"So where do cows go for fun?" Barney asked.

"Where?"

"The a-moo-sement park. Get it? A-moo-sement park? Moo-oo?"

"Yeah, yeah, I get it."

Finally, they arrived at a town called Ensenada. It looked like a tourist trap to Jacob. The dusty, unevenly paved streets were lined with dozens of souvenir shops and restaurants with big hand-painted signs in English. He leaned over Barney trying to peer out the side window. There were a few kids around, selling newspapers or just generally hanging out. But there were no parks, and no one kicking anything around, much less a soccer ball.

According to the guidebook, there were no campgrounds in town or close by, so Fred stopped the car at a small hotel on an especially gritty side street. When he and Jacob's mom went in to inquire about rooms, the kids all got out of the car and switched seats. Barney moved up to the front and Jacob took his place, sitting in the back by the window. Minerva moved to the back on the other side of Sam, who now sat in the middle.

They were all getting settled back in the car when four dark-haired young Mexican boys, none bigger than Jacob, drifted over. The boys wore dusty shorts and shirts, washed so often you had to guess their original colour. They stared at the car and said, "*Hola!*"

Jacob muttered, "*Hola,*" back to them. One of the boys tried to sell Barney a crumpled newspaper.

Barney shook his head. "No. No newspaper."

The boys pointed to the decorations on the storage box on the car's roof and smiled, thumbs up, nodding their approval. One boy, the tallest, pointed to the end of the box where Jacob had stuck the large soccer-ball sticker.

"*Futbol*," the boy said, grinning.

"*Futbol*," Jacob repeated, nodding.

The boy noticed Jacob's flattened ball on his knee. He reached inside the car and mischievously snatched up the ball.

"Hey, give that ball back," Jacob said, trying to grab it back.

"*Bueno futbol*," the boy said, smiling and patting the ball.

Jacob looked toward the hotel. No sign of his mom or Fred. They might be gone a long time. What should he do, he wondered. The boy seemed to like his ball even though it was flat. Maybe this was his chance to find a good home for his ball. It's true that he wanted to keep it forever, but like the guy in San Francisco had said, maybe this kid would patch up the ball and have his granny sew it up. Then it would be just like new again. The boy showed it to his friend. Or was it his brother?

"Ahh," the younger boy said appreciatively. "*Bueno futbol!*"

Staring at Jacob, the bigger boy stuffed the ball under his shirt, teasing him that he was stealing it.

"What's that guy doing, Jay?" Minerva said. "He's taking your ball!"

The boy took the ball out of his shirt and with his finger,

traced the penned name on the ball. "*Jelé … Jelé,*" he read, and it sounded to Jacob like "*Helé, Helé! Bravo Helé!*"

Jacob grinned at the boys. It was like he was some big-time soccer star with the boys all playing with his ball and chanting his name. He wanted to ask them where the nearest soccer game was. "*Donde esta el …*" he started, but his mom and Fred returned to the car.

"They don't have a room big enough for all six of us, but they told us about a motel at the edge of town not far from here," Jacob's mom said.

As the adults got into the car, the boy handed the ball back to Jacob.

"No," Jacob said, waving it back. "You can fix the ball. Your grandmother could sew it up. Then it would be just like new. A good ball for you. You can keep it. Really."

The boy looked puzzled. He pointed to himself and the ball and said something in Spanish so fast Jacob couldn't separate the sounds into words. Then he made out, "*Adiós, Jelé. Adiós, Jelé* Armstrong."

Then, as Jacob watched, the boy and his friends melted down the lane, empty-handed. "*Jelé, Jelé!*" The name echoed in his ears.

"Hey, you guys," Jacob shouted out his window. "Come back! Take the ball. You can have it! You can fix it! Your grandmother can sew it. Darn! I didn't even ask them where the soccer game was."

"That's a switch," his mother said. "Now you want to give your ball away?"

"At least they could play soccer with it. They could patch it and their grandmother could maybe sew it up," Jacob said. "If only I could find a soccer game."

"Maybe we'll see one on our way to the motel," his mother said.

But Jacob was out of luck. On their way to the motel, they didn't pass one park or even a vacant lot. There was no sign that soccer was played in this town. Or even in the whole country.

The motel at the edge of town had an inner courtyard surrounded by a high wall and thick bushes with clouds of pink flowers on them. It was really a parking lot, but not many cars were there.

It was a good place to kick a ball around, Jacob thought, appraising the good solid brick wall. His foot twitched. Then he glanced down at his battered ball. If only he had a good ball …

Fred parked the car beside the "Office" sign. He and Jacob's mother got out to find the manager. In a few minutes, a short plump woman wearing a large white apron over her black dress came out of the office, carrying a bundle of keys. Jacob's mother and Fred followed her, walking arm in arm.

Did they always have to walk like that? Jacob wondered. They were always touching, touching.

He found a round pebble about the size of his big toe.

He flicked it towards the brick wall, hard. It hit the wall and bounced back. He kicked it again before it stopped rolling. Kick, bounce, roll. Kick on the inside of the right foot, left foot. Vary the position with each kick. Kick hard. Now gently. Soft, soft. Down low, up. Ooh, that hurt the top of his foot, but it was a good kick. A strong one.

The motel had two adjoining units, one with a small room containing a large double bed, a single bed and a small bathroom. The other unit was the same except for a small kitchen with a wooden table, several chairs, a noisily humming refrigerator, and a big upside-down bottle of drinking water. When the tap was turned, water sprayed out of the bottom, as Barney soon discovered.

"Ooops," he said. His face turned red and he tried to smudge the puddle into the worn lino with his sandal. No one noticed except Jacob. Somehow it made him like … well, not exactly *like* Barney more, but think maybe he wasn't a complete nerd. Just clumsy and unlucky.

The following morning after an early breakfast of Cheerios and milk, Jacob said, "Now what I'd like to do is find a soccer game. There's got to be one happening, somewhere in this town."

His mother said, "All the boys will probably be just waking up so early in the morning. Why not come shopping with us? We might find something nice for you. Maybe even a brand new soccer ball."

They paraded, all six of them, down the sidewalk that led to the shopping district. Fred, with Sam hanging onto his arm, was in deep conversation with Barney, patiently answering one question after another. Jacob's mother walked slightly behind them.

Minerva, who was walking several paces behind her mother, pretended not to belong to the whole group. Jacob noticed her looking at several young tourists, all male, in fancy tourist clothes, with their hair slicked back and chests inflated. Did that one just wink at his sister? Was she smiling back, encouraging them, flirting with them?

Jacob placed himself right by Minerva's side. He didn't like the way those guys were staring at his sister, not one bit! How dare they!

"Minerva. Come on. Let's catch up with Mom."

"You can," she told him. "I'm not in any rush. This looks so much more interesting." She slowed her pace even more, lagging behind the others. She brushed back her dark hair and smiled again at one guy, flirting with him.

The teenager quickened his pace and fell in step right behind her.

"Come on, Min," Jacob urged. "We'll get lost."

Their mother and Fred had turned down another street and were out of sight now. For a frantic moment, Jacob didn't know what to do. He imagined those tall teenagers luring his sister into some dark corner. Then what? Maybe she'd run away with them? He had to think of something. And fast.

He started a comedy routine. If Barney could be a comedian, so could he. He made some moronic grunts and dragged one foot along the sidewalk, like a lame gorilla. That always made Minerva mad. It embarrassed her more than anything. He knew how much she hated walking beside him when he acted so stupid. He hunched his shoulders and flayed out his arms and grunted some more.

"Jacob!" she hissed. "Stop that or I'll slug you."

"Humph, humph!" he made loud gorilla noises back at her.

She frowned and walked faster to get away from him. His plan was working. He was embarrassing her all right. She walked even faster. He stayed right with her, dragging his foot and grunting. Now they were almost jogging. He continued his gorilla routine until they finally caught up with their mother.

"Oh, there you two are," she said. "I was wondering …"

"Mom. Can you tell Jacob to stop?"

"Stop what?" Jacob asked innocently, assuming his normal walk.

Minerva glowered at him, but Jacob didn't care. At least they had lost those creepy teenagers.

"Have you noticed these gorgeous shirts?" their mother said, stopping in front of a clothing and souvenir shop. Most shops along this street were clothing and souvenir shops. "These loose cotton ones. Lovely bright colours, don't you think? I'd like to get one for myself. And maybe one for Fred."

"Sure," Minerva said, turning away from Jacob to look at the display. "I'd like one too. They look cool."

"But Da-ad," Sam whined. "I *want* it. It says here that it's a Genuine Mexican Sombrero."

"It'll just get squashed in the car," Fred said.

"I'll look after it. I've always wanted a Real Genuine Mexican Sombrero," Sam said stubbornly.

"It's your money, I guess," Fred said, shaking his head.

Sam grinned. The hat was woven straw and had a wide brim with bright green pompoms all around and the crown was decorated with gaudy bead work.

How could anyone like it, Jacob wondered. Sam Finkle, king of tacky.

Jacob soon got bored watching Fred and Sam argue so he wandered down the aisle in the store. He didn't want anyone to think that he was with the Finkles. And he certainly didn't want to be with Minerva and his mother; they were prancing about in those bright cotton shirts and scarves like crazy birds of paradise. He hated shopping at the best of times. Shopping in this roasting store, with the glare of the blazing, sun-baked streets and the morning's sizzling heat pressing down on his shoulders, was making his head ache.

So this was Mexico. Pretty disappointing. Surely wasn't worth that long trip, cooped up in that smelly old car. Minerva had been right. They should have hopped a bus and headed for home a long time ago.

He noticed Barney standing at the door, idly kicking at the door frame with his heel. He wandered up to him.

"Talk about boring ..." Jacob said to him. "They don't even have a sports department."

Barney shrugged and followed Jacob out to the sidewalk. It was no cooler outside but at least the air smelled fresher.

Leaning against the storefront was a street vendor's display. It contained mostly silver jewelry and sunglasses.

"Hey, dig these," Jacob said. "The latest in cool shades." He pointed to a row of sunglasses.

"Wow! Genuine Oakleys with nuclear protection!" Barney exclaimed. "The real thing!"

"*Buenos días, amigos,*" a young man said, flashing them a wide smile. "You like the sunglasses? I give you very good price. Any pairs you see here for just twenty American dollars."

"Twenty dollars!" Barney said, shaking his head. "That's more than I've got."

"Make him an offer," Jacob said. "They're the latest. They're really cool."

"Ten dollars, I'll give you ten. I could use them in my act. You're right. They'd look so-o cool." He was staring hard and Jacob could almost see his mouth water.

"Ten dollars! That would give them away," the Mexican said. "Fifteen. I give them as a gift to you for fifteen dollars."

Barney pulled out his wallet. "I don't have fifteen. Look. Twelve dollars, That's it. That's all I have. Twelve American dollars." He opened his wallet and showed the vender two fives and two ones.

"Here. Try a pair. Any pair you see. Try on."

Barney chose a pair with fluorescent blue frames and technicolor lenses. He put them on over his glasses. The guy didn't have a mirror so he turned to Jacob.

"So, what do you think?"

"Cool," Jacob said. "They're real cool. And they cover your other glasses pretty well. Maybe I should get a pair too."

"I give you big bargain. Two pairs, twenty-five dollars."

Jacob hesitated. "No. I better save my money to buy a new ball. You give them to my, ah, friend here for twelve-fifty?"

The Mexican raised his hands. "Okay, okay. Twelve-fifty. Sold."

"Twelve-fifty will clean me out," Barney said, dumping out his wallet. "But for a pair of genuine Oakley wrap-arounds with nuclear protection, man oh man, it's worth it!"

He tried them without his normal glasses. "Can't see," he said. "Everything's too fuzzy." So he propped them onto his nose in front of his other glasses again.

Jacob started down the street looking for a sports store and Barney trailed after him, but in the whole shopping district, there was not a single sports store.

"This whole morning's one total waste of time," Jacob muttered. "If Mexico's supposed to be the land of soccer, where's the soccer?"

Eventually they rejoined Fred and Jacob's mom, and they did find a bakery. No doughnuts, but there was a pan of large delicious-smelling buns, fresh from the oven. Fred didn't want to buy any.

"We've got plenty of crackers back at the motel," he said.

"Eat crackers when we can have these delicious fresh buns?" Jacob's mother laughed. She bought a dozen and a large rosy-cheeked woman put them into two big paper bags.

As they trailed along the sidewalk, Jacob and Barney held back. They didn't want anyone to think they were with the funny little guy with the big sombrero decorated with pompoms. Talk about embarrassing!

The next morning, after taking photographs of their motel, they headed south through town. Jacob had to sit in the back of the car again, between Barney and Sam, who insisted on holding his precious sombrero on his lap.

"So it won't get squashed," he said. He tried to hold his whole packet of toys as well, all his little trucks and action figures. His stuff kept overflowing onto Jacob's knee and Jacob kept flicking it away. He felt like tossing the junk out the window. A lot of it ended up under their feet, littering the floor.

When the car halted at a stop light near the outskirts of town, a bunch of people were waiting to cross the street.

"Look!" Jacob said. "Isn't that the guy who grabbed my soccer ball?" Same hair, same size. The shirt was different maybe, but those greyish shorts with the raggedy bottoms were familiar.

Barney didn't even glance up from his joke book.

"That Mexican kid should have kept my ball," Jacob

muttered. "Then he'd probably be off somewhere right now with his friends playing with it, all patched and pumped up. I bet they'd be passing it back and forth, then whack! Into the net for a goal. Then they'd raise their hands over their heads and dance around the field, yelling, 'Jelé, Jelé!'"

"Yeah, yeah," Barney said. "Here's a good one. What has one horn and gives milk?"

"What?"

"A milk truck."

Jacob groaned. As the car started up again, he leaned over Sam to get a better look at the boy at the crosswalk.

"Hey!" Sam squealed. "You're squashing my new hat!"

"Sorry," Jacob mumbled.

The boy was gone now. Was it really the same one? He couldn't be sure.

13

Right away, Jacob could tell the camp was a dump. It wasn't a chain like the KOA or anything. It didn't have a pool or even a games room. It's true that there was a river, a bubbling and boiling whitewater stream that made Fred groan with pleasure.

"Can't wait to run that water in the kayak," he said.

Jacob's mother protested. "Oh, Fred! But it looks too dangerous! Look at all those rocks. And the water's so swift."

"It's nothing compared to the Chilliwack and we run that all the time."

The sign was in English. "Welcome to Camp Solo," it said. "Camping, rafting and natural hot springs."

"Hot springs," Jacob's mother sighed. "Now *that* sounds wonderful."

That settled it. They would stay the night, camping under one of the dusty trees. At least the village wasn't too far away. Jacob could take a walk later and check it out, maybe find a video arcade. Maybe even a park with a soccer game happening. The only other kids he saw were some teenagers bobbing down the river on inner tubes and different kinds of inflatable objects. They looked like they were having a whale of a time, but there wasn't a single soccer ball in sight.

He and Minerva had their tent up on the packed ground in a couple of minutes. They were so used to setting it up now, they could do it blindfolded.

He got his ball out of his pack and headed down to the river to see if there was a good wall he could kick it against. Although it was lopsided and wobbled all over the place, at least it was something he could kick. And it didn't hurt his toes as much as a rock did.

Down near the river was a cleared area of short dry grass, but there wasn't any wall or even a large rock to kick his ball against. If only there was a kid he could play with. He'd even settle for clumsy old Barney. But Barney was off with Fred, fiddling with the kayak.

Jacob bounced the ball on his instep and passed it lightly from foot to foot. Sam had followed him down to the river. He stood on the bank, wearing that stupid sombrero, and stared at the water splashing and tumbling over the rocks.

"Hey, want to kick the ball around a while?" Jacob asked him. Even El Shrimpo was better than no one.

"Who me?" Sam said. "Sure!"

Jacob gently passed him the ball. It wobbled toward his feet. Sam fumbled over his feet, but managed to make contact and kick it back, sort of.

Jacob kicked it to him again, a little stronger this time. Sam kicked the ball back to him. Back and forth they went.

Sam grinned and squealed every time his feet made contact with the ball, and the pompoms on his hat bounced crazily.

Jacob began to think that maybe with practice, a lot of practice, this Finkle kid might actually learn how to play soccer.

Sam kicked the ball extra hard. But the ball, instead of wobbling back to Jacob, bounced down the slope and into the river!

Jacob skidded down the slope after it, but Sam was closer.

"I'll get it!" Sam shouted, jumping into the bubbling stream. He grabbed at the ball, but lost his balance. He tumbled down onto his knees in the water and his sombrero fell off. It was swept away and was caught between two rocks.

"My sombrero!" he sputtered, struggling to get up. The swirling stream tugged him in and he floundered about in the bubbling water.

On the bank, Jacob hesitated an instant. Should he go for his ball, or Sam and the dumb hat?

"Hold on there, kid!" he yelled, plunging into the water. He gasped as it splashed cool around his legs and tugged him off balance. He spread his feet wide and leaned upstream against the current. Sam was thrashing his arms about. Jacob lunged out, grabbed Sam's T-shirt and hauled him up, gasping and coughing.

"Got you, kid," he muttered.

"My hat!" Sam wheezed.

Jacob lunged again and caught the twirling sombrero with the other hand. The water boiled and crashed around them, pushing them downstream, but Jacob's fingers were locked firmly around Sam's shirt and his hat.

He took a step toward the bank and tripped on a loose rock. He gasped and sprawled to his knees, splashing into the water up to his chin, but he didn't let go. Coughing and spitting out water, he pulled himself up and towed the kid and the hat toward the riverbank again. Then he shoved Sam into the shallows near some big rocks.

"Hang on tight to those rocks!" he shouted.

His ball was twirling crazily in the current, bashing against one big rock and then another. He lunged toward it, but before he could get near, it was swept away downstream, out of sight.

Sam seemed to be losing his grip on the rocks so Jacob pushed his way back through the water and caught him. He dragged him and his stupid sombrero out of the shallow water and safely up the bank. When he turned back to scan the river for his ball again, it was gone.

Beside him, Sam was wheezing and sputtering still, coughing and choking out the water. Jacob gently patted the little guy's back until he finally caught his breath.

"You okay now?" he asked.

Sam sniffled and rubbed his nose on the back of his hand. He took a deep breath and nodded. He looked up at Jacob, his eyes shining. "You saved me, Jay. You're like a — a super hero on TV. You saved me! I could a drowned in there."

Jacob shook his head. "Not really, kid. The water's not all that deep." The way the little kid was staring up at him was embarrassing, but it made him feel so tall. Tall and kind of powerful.

"But your ball, Jay. S-sorry I kicked it into the river. Your ball's really gone this time."

"It's okay, kiddo." Jacob was feeling strangely unconcerned about his ball. He knew his father would agree that he'd made the right choice, going for the kid instead of trying to rescue his ball. At least the kid was safe. "The ball really wasn't much good any more. Some Mexican kid, like the one we saw yesterday, will probably fish it out of the river downstream. Then he can patch it and ask his granny to stitch it up really fine. Then he'll use it to play soccer with all his friends."

"You really think so, Jay?" Sam said, following him back to their campsite.

"Sure. I'm sure that's exactly what will happen. Now you better get into some dry clothes. At least now you don't have to worry about washing those."

"Whatever happened to you two?" Jacob's mother asked as they approached. She was sitting on a camp chair in the shade with her book.

"I fell into the river, and Jacob, he came in after me," Sam said, water dripping down his legs. "And he rescued me. He did."

"Really! What were you doing in the river?"

"I went in after Jacob's ball," Sam said. "But it's lost down the river now."

"Is that so?" Jacob's mother asked Jacob.

Jacob shrugged. "I tried to grab it too, but couldn't get to it on time."

"Well, you two better get changed out of those wet clothes. Here are a couple of towels."

"So Jacob's like a hero on TV, isn't he?" Sam said, sniffing and wiping his nose on his wet shirt.

"He's a hero, all right," Jacob's mother said. "And I'm proud of him." She smiled warmly at Jacob.

"No big deal," Jacob muttered as he ducked under his towel.

Later that afternoon, Jacob was sitting on the picnic table, idly swishing a branch back and forth. Barney was sitting beside him, with his new Oakley wrap-arounds perched on the end of his nose. Barney wiggled his nose to see if the glasses would stay on. They didn't. They slipped down and he shoved them back up again.

"Minerva and I are making supper tonight," Jacob's mother said. She was wearing a long silky scarf of blue, green and yellow around her head. Must be one of her new ones, thought Jacob. "So while you two sweeties are hanging around, how about walking into the village for some milk? And maybe some fresh fruit, if you can find any."

Jacob put his mother's change purse with some of his own pesos into his pocket and set out towards the village with Barney.

"Hope this joint at least has a video arcade," Jacob said to him.

"Knock, knock," Barney said.

"Okay. Who's there?"

"Cows go."

"Cows go who?"

"No, cows go moo."

"Okay, here's another one to add to your collection," Jacob said. "Knock, knock."

"Who's there?"

"Moo-moo."

"Moo-moo who?"

"Make up your mind. Are you a cow or an owl?"

"Hey, I like that one. Just a sec," Barney said, fishing in his pocket. "I want to write it down in my notebook. Now, can I try out my opening act on you again? There's this man, see. Out riding his horse and he gets lost, see. And he comes to this old lady who's leading a cow ..."

The village didn't have anything like a video arcade. There were a couple of shops bordering the dusty road, a hardware store and a gas station connected to a restaurant that advertised GAZ and TACOS. Next to it sat a general store in an old building with peeling grey paint and a large Coca-Cola sign.

"We should find milk in here," Jacob told Barney.

The store sold everything you could imagine. Tins of food and boxes of soap powder were packed neatly along the shelves, and there was a row of candy and gum that drew Barney like a magnet. A lot of the stuff was marked in American dollars. Probably for the tourists.

"Obviously no video arcade in town so we may as well get some gum," Jacob said.

After choosing a package of Spearmint, he left Barney drooling over the six different flavours of bubble gum. He went down the next aisle towards the back of the store and Barney soon followed him.

"Wow!" said Barney. "Will you take a look at those!"

There was a pile of large, brightly coloured inflatable beach toys.

"So?"

"Look, there's a cow! A purple cow! 'I've never seen a purple cow, but I'd rather see than be one!'" he quoted.

The vinyl cow was huge and purple with big brown eyes and a floppy tail. Standing on its skinny inflated legs, it was almost up to their shoulders.

"Oh, I've *got* to have this cow!" Barney moaned. "Just think what a difference it would make to my act if I had that!"

"But what would you do with it?"

"It would be part of my routine. Also, I bet you could get two guys on any one of these and whip down the river by our camp. They're obviously for running the river. They're made out of really heavy vinyl. Man, oh, man! That would be such a gas! Twenty bucks, though. There's no way I could afford that. These Oakley's pretty well cleaned me out." He stroked the cow's back as if it were a real animal.

Jacob nodded. He continued down the aisle toward the

milk cooler. Then he saw it! He gasped. A cardboard box with familiar green and black writing on it. He reached up and grabbed the box. "Yes!" he muttered, his heart leaping. "It is! It's a genuine SUPARI soccer ball! Exactly like the one my dad gave me!" He could feel his face splitting with a grin. He smelled the ball. It had the good familiar aroma of leather. He carefully pulled it out of the box and stroked its smooth sides. It was firm and unblemished. He dropped it to the top of his foot to feel its weight. Perfect! He flicked it up and hugged it close. Then he gently slipped it back into its box. He returned it to the shelf, taking note of how many pesos it was. He hadn't spent much so he had more than thirty dollars left of his holiday money. So maybe, just maybe, he had enough to buy it.

"Come on," he said to Barney, who was still drooling over the purple cow. "We'd better get the milk and stuff and get back to camp before it gets dark." That's one thing he'd noticed about this place. As soon as the sun went down just after six, it became pitch dark. Just like what Minerva had told him it was like in Jamaica.

All the way back along the road, Barney jabbered on about that inflatable purple cow. "Hey, Jay. You ever run a river?"

Jacob shook his head. "No. Don't really like water all that much. Unless it's in a bathtub."

"How could anyone not like water?"

Jacob just shrugged in his direction.

"Last summer," Barney told him, "Sam and I went down the Chilliwack River in a rubber raft with my dad. We got almost to the end, over these huge rapids, then we dumped. The water sure was cold, but man oh man! It was the greatest! Whipping down those chutes! Better than a roller coaster any day. Even better than that dune buggy ride we had in Oregon."

"Hey, I didn't tell you. Know what I saw at that store in the village?"

"What?"

"A really prize soccer ball. Just like my old one. Gonna buy it tomorrow if I've got enough money."

"Yeah? How much have you got left?"

"Thirty bucks from my vacation fund."

"Lucky. All I've got for the rest of this trip is a bit of change. But I guess these Oakley's are worth it. They're really cool. But if I had enough money, I'd get me one of those cows. What a gas it would be! Just think what a difference it would make to my act. And running down the river on it. That would be the best!"

A supper of chili, tacos and salad was ready when they returned.

"Hey, this isn't half bad," Barney said, loading cheese and salsa onto his taco. "Maybe I'm getting used to all this foreign food."

"Food always tastes better when you're hungry," Jacob's mother said. She didn't have to coax Jacob to eat. He was into his fifth taco already. Yum!

"I found the hot springs," Fred said. "They're upstream in a rather small pool coming out of a cave. Stuck my foot in and it's a tad hot, but not unpleasant. The camp owner said they plan to develop it one of these days but they haven't yet. How would you fancy a dip after supper?"

It was too dark for a trip back to the village after supper, and the general store would probably be closed, so Jacob couldn't go back to buy the Supari soccer ball. He got his towel and bathing suit and they all followed Fred along the path upstream, armed with flashlights against the gloom. They passed a small dance pavilion with a sign. They flashed their lights on it and read, "Cha-cha lessons tomorrow morning, 10:00."

"Ooh, Fred," Jacob's mother said, squeezing his arm. "I love the cha-cha-cha!"

"Right-o. You can teach me tomorrow," he said patting her hand and smiling down at her.

The moon came out and lit the steamy water, which gurgled from a dark cave into a small pool surrounded by rocks. Water spilled over the rocks into the river. A faint odour of old eggs floated up with the steam, but it wasn't strong enough to be unpleasant.

"It's the sulphur in the water," Fred explained.

Jacob slowly lowered himself into the hot pool. The water was as warm as a hot bath and came almost to his chin. His skin tingled but after a while he felt his muscles relaxing. Minerva sighed as she sank down beside him. For once she didn't have music blaring away. She wasn't even plugged into her headphones. Sam hovered near Fred, who had his arm around Jacob's mother.

"Blimey!" Fred said. "Now, this is the life!" He stretched out his long hairy legs and wiggled his toes.

Jacob's mother leaned her head on his shoulder and smiled up at him.

Jacob felt a small pang, but his mother looked so happy that it made him smile too.

Steaming water trickled over a rocky edge to the river below.

Barney said to Jacob, "You know what would be really fun! We could dive down into the river from this ledge."

"Oh, no, you don't, young man," Fred said. "You could crack your head on the rocks. There's no way of knowing how deep that water in the river is."

"Could we climb down the rocks and check it out?"

"Fine, but be careful," Fred said.

"Want to, Jay?" Barney asked.

Jacob felt as if he was starting to dissolve in the hot water so the thought of a cool water dip was enticing. "Okay. I'll come with you," he said.

The river water swirled coolly around his chest. Sam and Minerva soon followed Jacob and Barney. Sam was telling Minerva all about the movie *Tarzan*, and demonstrating the different swimming strokes from the movie. Minerva watched him with great interest, grinning and encouraging him. She seemed to be actually enjoying the story.

Jacob dived underwater and let the coolness flow past his face and through his hair. He swam underwater until his lungs were bursting. He shot up to the surface, and sprayed like a fountain, like a dolphin.

When Barney asked him if he wanted to go back up to the hot pool, Jacob agreed and followed him, clambering up the slippery, rocky bank. His mother and Fred were still in the pool, arms clasped around each other. They were kissing.

Again, Jacob felt a pang, but he raised his eyebrows and grinned at Barney and they splashed noisily into the hot water.

Jacob's mother let go of Fred and smiled at them. "So, my sweets," she said. "How's the water down there?"

"Refreshing," Jacob said. "You two should try it."

Fred followed Jacob's mother over the ledge and down to the river, leaving the hot pool to Barney and Jacob. Now they could stretch out full-length in the hot water and rest their heads on the rocky ledge. In the silence, they gazed up at the stars, which looked like bright pinpricks in the dark velvet sky.

"Mushy honeymooners," Jacob said.

"Yeah," Barney said. "All that kissing and stuff. Yuck! Wonder why they have to do that so much."

"Guess it's all part of it," Jacob told him. Their legs looked like four long sausages rippling under the dark water. "Hey, Barney, let me ask you something. What about your mom? How often do you see her?"

Barney drew in a long breath. "We don't see her all that much," he said. "We got divorced when I was a little kid, around five. I don't remember much about when we were all together. We all went on a picnic once. I remember that. It was so cold and wet that we froze. Not much fun. Sam and me, we go over to her place sometimes on the weekends but I always get the feeling that she's not too sad when we have to leave. At least she doesn't complain. Know what I mean?"

Jacob nodded. He was lying there, the warm water lapping around his ears. The night was quiet and still. No breeze. No traffic noises. The odd flutter from an insect, or was it a night bird? Or a bat, maybe? He couldn't tell. A tranquil murmur of voices drifted up from the river. He breathed deeply and stared at the star-plastered sky. If he could have reached up and touched the sky, he was sure it would have felt as smooth as glass. As smooth as that brand new Supari soccer ball he was going to get tomorrow. The air was thick purple darkness. The constellations hummed like halogen lamps.

Peace. A feeling of deep contentment seeped into him.

14

The next morning Jacob turned over in his sleeping bag and stared at the tent wall. He woke up thinking about the ball he had seen the day before at the store in the village. He remembered walking towards the milk cooler. And there it was. His ball! The exact replica of the one his father had given him. The one he'd lost in the river. A hand-stitched, genuine World Cup Supari. His heart leapt against his ribs like a wild bird trying to escape.

He remembered that he had reached up and gently, oh, so gently, pulled the ball from its box. It was firm and smooth. No cracks or scars. It was unblemished. Perfect. Oh, the smell! The pure leather smell! He could smell it now. How he longed to kick the ball! He had gently pushed it along with his toe, had caught it up in his arms. He had embraced it and smelled it again, inhaling long and deeply.

He had figured out that the ball cost just over twenty-five American dollars. He still had thirty dollars left, so today that ball, that beautiful, perfect ball was going to be his!

Minerva nudged him with her foot. "Hey, Jay. You awake yet?"

He stretched his arms out over his head. "Why? What do you want?"

"It's Barney's birthday today. We still haven't got him anything. Any ideas?"

Jacob rolled over and peered at his sister through sleepy eyes. She was sitting on her sleeping bag already dressed, brushing out her long thick hair. Must be later than he thought. The sun had already brightened the blue sides of their tent.

"I know what he'd like," he told her.

"What?"

"There's this stupid-looking inflatable purple cow we saw yesterday at the village general store. He went all gaga over it. Said he could run the river on it, and also use it in his cow act."

"Great! Let's get it for him."

"Just a minute. It costs twenty bucks. Plus tax. Not exactly cheap."

"So? You can afford it. You've still got most of your trip money, don't you?"

"Yes, but I'm buying a new ball with it. How about you pay for the cow and I'll pay you back when we get home?"

"No way! Where am I going to get that kind of money? I have less than ten dollars of my trip money left." Minerva pulled a clip through her hair and tied it back into a pony-tail. "We could get him some other cheaper present. But we have to hurry because Mom said we're going to celebrate his birthday at breakfast time. That's when they always do it. She said Fred told her the boys don't like waiting all day until supper so they always have their birthday at breakfast time. Weird, eh?"

"Weird," Jacob said. "But not such a bad idea."

Their mother was at the picnic table getting the camp stove started to make tea. The rays from the early morning sun glinted off the kettle. "Good morning." Her smile greeted them. "It's Fred's day for cooking and he's going to make us his specialty, pancakes, which is Barney's favourite breakfast."

"We're thinking about walking into the village to get a birthday present for him," Minerva said.

"Great! You could go now. Fred's gone for a kayak paddle down the river so breakfast will be a while. Have an orange or something. Maybe you could pick up some more milk. We're already pretty low."

"They've got a soccer ball there, Mom, at the store. Real leather with hand stitching. A genuine Supari like my old one. A beaut! I want to get that too."

"That's wonderful!" his mother smiled at him. "I'm glad you finally found one."

The storekeeper was unlocking the door when they arrived. He was an American with long brown hair in a ponytail and a round pot belly.

Jacob led the way to the sports section. "Yes!" he said. "It's still here!" His ball was up on the top shelf where he'd left it the evening before. He reached for it.

"Looks great," Minerva agreed. "So where are those purple cows you were talking about?"

"Down there," Jacob said, pointing with his elbow.

When Minerva saw the cows, she laughed. "You're right, Jay! Barney would be crazy about one of those. I can just see him bouncing down the river. He'd absolutely love one!"

"I know he would."

Yes. The ball felt as smooth and firm as he remembered. He stroked it with his chin and inhaled the good leather aroma. Oh, how his foot itched to kick it! His toes spread apart in his running shoes. He squeezed them back together.

"Twenty dollars," Minerva said. "That would be just ten bucks each, plus tax."

"Told you, I don't have enough. This ball's twenty-five, probably twenty-six with tax. All I'll have then is about four dollars, unless you pay my part. Like I said, I could pay you back when we get home."

"And I told you, I don't have any extra cash at all. Ten bucks will pretty well break me."

"Can I help you?" the storekeeper asked.

"We're trying to decide on a present," Minerva told him.

The man nodded. "That's my best ball you got there," he said to Jacob. "Last one in stock. Don't know if I can get any more in. Got another one, though. Half the price, but not genuine leather. Not Mexican. Imported." He moved a couple of boxes around on the shelf and showed Jacob another soccer ball. It was a shiny white and red one, size 5, regulation sized.

Jacob put the leather ball back on the shelf and felt the plastic one with his fingertips. His nose wrinkled at the sharp artificial smell. The surface was smooth, no stitching to come undone, he told himself. But he had kicked balls like this one before. Although they were supposedly the same size and weight as the real ones, the leather, hand-stitched ones, kicking them was never the same. Not the same feel, not the same satisfying sound.

"You could buy that one and still afford half the cow for Barney," Minerva said, persuasively. "You've got thirty dollars, right?"

Jacob nodded. He took one last look at the leather, hand-stitched black and white Supari in its shiny black and green box. He'd probably never see one of those again, but it was true, Barney would love that stupid inflated purple cow so much. He was so crazy about water and also, it would give his comedy routine a real focus.

And this plastic ball wasn't really so bad. If you didn't look too closely, that is.

Standing at the cash register with the plastic ball in his hands, Jacob found he couldn't look at it at all. With its false shine, its bright red design, its phony smell, it was just plain embarrassing.

The shopkeeper rang up the inflated cow and the ball. "And with the tax, that comes to …"

"Um. Just a minute," Jacob decided. "Changed my mind about the ball. Not going to take it after all."

The shopkeeper nodded, understanding. "That other one sort of spoils you for anything else now, don't it?"

"Don't look so glum," Minerva said on their way back to camp. "You've still got twenty dollars."

"Might as well be zero," he grumbled. "When what you need is twenty-six bucks and all you got is twenty, it might as well be zero. Sure you can't lend me a measly six bucks?"

"You'd need at least that with the tax. And I just don't have it. I've got less than a dollar now to last me all the way home. And that's for two weeks."

They each took an end of the cow and carried it on their shoulders. It wasn't heavy, just awkward with its long skinny legs and floppy tail, dangling down their backs.

"Hey," Minerva said. "I just thought of a cow joke."

"Oh, no! Not you too!" Jacob groaned.

"What's the best way to raise a cow?"

"What?"

"Hold onto its head and tail and lift!"

"That's so bad," Jacob groaned again. "Just don't tell it to Barney."

They walked on for awhile and he said, "Sure wish we hadn't made that deal with Mom to give us money at the beginning of the trip on condition that we don't ask for any more during the whole trip."

"She's trying to make us financially responsible. Remember?"

"Think she'd lend me six bucks?"

"I wouldn't even bother asking."

"What about Fred?"

"He's even worse. Frugal Fred Finkle, remember?"

15

Barney whooped for joy when he saw the purple cow. Although Jacob and Minerva tried disguising it under an orange tarp, he guessed right away what it was.

"Wow! I don't believe it! Wow! It's so terrific! Wow! It's the best present I've ever had in my whole entire life! Thanks, guys." He put his arm around the cow and hugged it like a pet dog.

Jacob nodded and grinned at him.

Barney's eyes behind his glasses were so bright they were glittering like Halloween sparklers. His red hair stood out in spikes. "Can I go and try it out in the river now?" he asked. "Can I? Can I?"

"I thought pancakes were your favourite," Fred said, brandishing the pancake flipper over the frying pan.

"They are, they are."

"Well, my pancakes can't wait all day and the river can, so eat up and you can play later."

After breakfast, Jacob and Minerva, Barney and Sam got into their bathing suits and rubber sandals and trailed down to the river to launch the purple cow. Several teenagers were already swooping down the river on various kinds of inflatable toys, inner tubes, rubber rafts, whirling around in the shallow water, laughing like crazy.

Fred got into his kayak to supervise. He had insisted that Barney wear a life jacket.

Barney tied on the life jacket and dropped the cow in at the edge of the river. Sand weights in the cow's feet kept it upright in the shallow water. Straddling its back, he pushed into deeper water and the current twirled the cow so now Barney faced upstream. "Yahoo!" he yelled, twirling round and round, waving his arm. "Yahoo!" It was like he was on the back of a bucking bronco. The current grabbed him and whirled him downstream. "Yahoo!"

"Watch those bloomin' big rocks!" Fred yelled. "And get out before the rapids!"

Jacob jogged along the bank, trailing Barney who was bouncing and twirling downstream. At an especially bubbly section, the cow flipped him into the water and he came up gasping.

"Man, oh man!" he sputtered. "That's the best!"

Reaching from his kayak, Fred caught the cow by its tail before it could drift away downstream. Barney grabbed it from him and pulled it through the shallow water to shore.

Jacob helped Barney haul the cow along the sandy river-bank, back up to the starting place.

Barney was smiling a smile as wide as his face could hold. "Man! That's so great! Even better than a giant roller coaster, I bet."

"I want a turn," Sam said, jumping around. "Can I, Barney? Can I have a turn? Please, please, please?"

Barney said, "I think this time either Jacob or Minerva should go since it was their present."

"You go ahead, Jay," Minerva said.

"Want to come down with me?" Jacob asked Barney. "Think it could hold both of us?"

"Sure. Let's try it."

"Just a minute," Fred said. "You better wear a life jacket too, Jacob. There's another one in the car."

Minerva got it and Jacob buckled it on and splashed into the water after Barney. The water swirled around his thighs as he straddled the cow's back and tried to hold onto its head, which was wobbling all over the place. Barney sat behind him and grabbed onto his waist.

"We need some reins or something to hold onto this guy," Jacob said.

"Don't worry, Jay. Hold on with your knees. If you do fall off, the water's not that deep."

As they took off, Jacob grabbed fistfuls of plastic cow ears and held on for dear life.

The current whirled them around and tugged them downstream. The riverbank was a blur, they were travelling so fast. Jacob's stomach lurched and dove as they slid past big rocks, shiny with spray. "Yippee!" he yelled.

"Ride 'em, cowboy!" Barney yelled as they surged through the foaming water, down towards the rapids, twirling round and round, water splashing up into their faces and hair.

They were almost at the bottom of the run near the bend when they realized they could control their path by leaning together one way or another.

"The rapids! We got to get out of here!" Barney hollered. "Lean left! Lean left!" They both leaned too far. The cow flipped, spilling them into the shallow water. Jacob came up sputtering. He grabbed the cow by the tail and laughed, spitting up water. Barney grabbed the head and they both hauled the cow through the bubbling water to the bank. They scrambled up the rocks, and hoisting the cow to their shoulders, they carried it back to the launching place, the wet tail dripping into Jacob's face.

"You get the soccer ball at the store?" Barney asked on the way.

"I didn't have enough money." Jacob shook his head. "But I don't want to think about it. Someone else has probably already bought it anyway. The shopkeeper said it was his last one."

"So how much do you need?"

"Six, maybe seven bucks with the tax."

"Ask your mom for a loan, why don't you?"

"Can't. That was part of the deal. She gave Minerva and me forty bucks at the beginning of the trip and we had to give her our word that we wouldn't ask her for any more money. No matter what."

"And all you need is six or seven bucks? I've got an idea where you might get some money."

"Where?

"You know those guys going down the river on rafts and tubes and stuff?"

"Yeah."

"Upstream, where they launch, I saw a whole pile of empty pop cans and bottles. People just chuck them out. They don't even bother about recycling."

"Yeah, but six or seven dollars worth? That's a lot of cans. I don't know …"

Sam pounced on Barney when they got back.

"My turn now. Right, Barney?"

"Sure. You want to go down with him, Min?"

"Love to," she said.

"Just be sure to get out at the bend. You don't want to go down those rapids."

Minerva nodded.

"Where's Mom?" Jacob asked.

"She and Fred left for a walk up the river." She pointed with her chin. "To the dance pavilion so she can teach Fred how to cha-cha-cha."

"Teach my dad to cha-cha!" Barney said. "That's a laugh!

Sometimes he can't even walk straight without falling over."

Jacob and Barney gave Minerva and Sam the life jackets so they could buckle them on before carrying the cow into the shallow water. They climbed on the cow's back, Sam in front and Minerva behind him, holding him on securely.

"*Adiós amigos*," Minerva shouted as they took off, the current swirling them away.

Jacob waved, then turned to see Fred and his mother strolling arm in arm along a path near the riverbank. Fred was wearing a colourful cotton shirt Jacob had never seen before. Probably his mother had bought it for him.

"Lovebirds," Barney snorted.

"Yeah," Jacob agreed. "Lovebird honeymooners." He felt the corners of his mouth twitch into a grin. He was sort of getting used to seeing them arm in arm like that all the time. "So you want to take a look for those bottles?"

When they went upstream they found that the riverbank was littered with garbage as well as empty bottles and cans. They picked up as many as they could. There were still a lot more so they went back to the car for a couple of big plastic garbage bags. They put the beer and pop cans into one bag and the bottles into the other. When they were finished poking through the garbage, Fred and Jacob's mother had returned from their dancing lesson. They still had their arms wrapped around each other and they were laughing.

"Oh, Barney, you should see your father dance!" Jacob's mother said. "We'll turn him into a true Jamaican yet."

And they demonstrated the dance steps while Jacob's mom sang, "Cha-cha-cha."

Fred was actually giggling. The tails of his new shirt, a wild blue and yellow print, swayed as he twirled, wiggling his behind and snapping his fingers in the air.

Jacob and Barney laughed at them.

"We're taking these bottles up to the store in the village," Jacob said when the dancing demonstration was over.

"Don't be long," his mother said, wiping her glowing forehead with her scarf. "Check-out time is 1:00 and we still have to take down the tents and pack up."

The boys put on dry T-shirts and shorts and Barney got his Oakley wrap-arounds and they set off.

The bag with the bottles was heavy. Jacob hadn't known that stale pop and beer got a sour smell, like mouldy apples. It was sort of sickening. Jacob and Barney alternated carrying the lighter tin bag and the heavier bottle bag. On the way, they checked garbage cans and found a few more cans and bottles.

"Think that's enough now?"

"Must be. Weighs a ton."

The closer they got to the store, the faster Jacob walked. As they approached the old grey building, he was almost running. He was going to get that soccer ball after all! What if it was already sold? No, it couldn't be! Maybe someone was there, right this very minute, paying for it.

Or maybe someone was on his way to the store with money in hand. Jacob's mouth was dry. He swallowed and wiped his sweaty forehead with the back of his hand.

"Holy smokes," Barney panted beside him. "Wait up!"

"We've got to hurry!" Jacob said. He broke into a jog and the bag of bottles banged against his leg.

The shopkeeper was totalling a woman's groceries at the cash register when they burst into the store. He winked at Jacob. "Thought you'd be back."

Jacob dashed to the sports section. He searched the shelves. Where was it? Was it still up on the shelf in its black box? Yes! Relief! Relief! The ball had not been sold. He lifted it down from the shelf as gently as he would a baby. He took it out of the box.

World Cup Supari. Leather as smooth and firm as ever. Exactly the right size and weight. His fingers traced the hand stitching. You couldn't beat that real leather smell. It was exactly like the ball his father had given him. Exactly like that one.

After the shopkeeper had packed the woman's groceries, given her change and bid her *adiós*, he turned his attention to the boys.

"So, *amigos*. What can I do for you?"

Jacob held up his bag. "We want to cash in these pop bottles and cans."

The man's dark eyes widened. "Sorry, guys." He shook his head sadly. "We don't give money for old bottles and cans. Not like in the States. There's no recycling here in Mexico."

Jacob's heart sank. It hadn't even occurred to him that in Mexico there was no refund for returning cans. So he wouldn't be getting the ball after all.

"Well, um, I …" His throat tightened. Here it was. The ball. Right here in his hands. His eyes blurred up so he could hardly see it. He blinked hard, and slowly slipped the ball back into its box. Then he stumbled back down the aisle to return it to the shelf.

"Say, Mister," Barney said. "These sunglasses. How much could you give me for them? They're real genuine Oakleys. I paid twelve-fifty American for them just the other day. They're still practically brand new."

"Twelve American dollars? Nice glasses," the shopkeeper said, examining them. "They're the latest craze with teens these days but I don't know if I could go as high as twelve dollars. I could maybe give you eight?"

"Eight dollars? Okay. It's a deal. Hey, Jay. Now we've got enough for that ball."

Jacob rubbed his eyes on his wrists and turned around. Barney offered him a fistful of crumpled American dollar bills.

"But — but your glasses, Barney. You liked them so much. They're genuine Oakleys. You don't want to sell them."

"Ah, they didn't really fit that great anyway. Kept falling off. Take the money. You can pay me back when we get home. I know where you'll be living." He grinned and pushed up his old wire-framed glasses.

"If you're sure. Thanks a lot, Barn." Jacob grinned back. "So now I owe you."

"Let's hurry and get back to camp," Barney said. "I want to get in a couple more runs down the river on that purple cow before we have to take off."

Jacob leaned his head against the back seat rest. He was almost drunk with the sharp leather smell of his new soccer ball. He hugged it to his chest. They were driving through the village heading north back to the States, and he was sitting in the back seat between Barney and Sam.

Sam was staring out his window and singing softly, "Oh, the old grey mare, she ain't what she used to be ..." Pretty good singer for a little kid, thought Jacob.

Jacob's mother turned around from the front seat and smiled back at them. "So two more weeks and we'll be home. How's it going, my sweeties? All comfortable back there?"

Without missing a beat in his humming, Sam nodded yes. Barney was almost asleep. He hadn't told a single cow joke since they had started out. Those last runs down the river on the purple cow had exhausted him. Jacob was going to have to figure out how to keep him exhausted all the time, for the rest of the trip.

He stroked his new ball and grinned back at his mother. "Great holiday, Mom. A really great holiday."

Barney's head bounced lightly against Jacob's shoulder. It didn't feel too uncomfortable.

There was no way he'd ever consider Barney a brother, or even a half-brother. Step-brother? No, that didn't fit either.

But friend, yeah. Maybe friend felt all right. My friend. That's what he'd called him a couple of days ago to the street vendor.

Maybe he could even teach Barney and the humming squirt how to kick a soccer ball properly, without it ending up in the river. It was possible that they could learn. After all, it looked like they were going to be spending a lot of time together.

May as well make the best of it.

ACKNOWLEDGEMENTS

I would like to thank my family who did that first trip all the way to Mexico and not only survived, but inspired this story. I would also like to thank my fellow writers, Jim Heneghan and Sonia Craddock, for their insightful comments and encouragement after reading many early drafts of the novel.

ABOUT THE AUTHOR

All the Way to Mexico is Norma Charles' thirteenth book for young readers. Among her previous books are the best-selling *See You Later, Alligator* (Scholastic, 1991), *Sophie Sea to Sea* (Beach Holme, 1999) and *The Accomplice* (Raincoast, 2001), which was shortlisted for a BC Book Prize and was also a Children's Book Centre "Our Choice" selection. Norma lives in Vancouver and writes fulltime. *All the Way to Mexico* is loosely based on a trip she and her family took several years ago.